Santa Paws, Come Home

D1351883

Nicholas Edwards

SCHOLASTIC

For Zack

The best ever.

Scholastic Children's Books,
Commonwealth House,
1–19 New Oxford Street,
London WC1A 1NU, UK
a division of Scholastic Ltd
London ~ New York ~ Toronto ~ Sydney ~ Auckland
Mexico City ~ New Delhi ~ Hong Kong

First published in the US by Scholastic Inc., 1999
Published in the UK by Scholastic Ltd, 2000

Text copyright © Ellen Emerson White, 1999

ISBN 0 439 99721 6

Typeset by TW Typesetting, Midsomer Norton, Somerset

Printed by Cox & Wyman Ltd, Reading, Berks.

2 4 6 8 10 9 7 5 3 1

Chapter 1

It was a cold December afternoon, and the dog was very happy. Actually, the dog was almost *always* happy, but today had been particularly nice. He had gone outside in the garden a few times, he had eaten three Milk-Bones, and he had just finished the latest in a long series of naps. Even better, the family cat, Evelyn, had not hissed at him at all today!

The house was full of wonderful places to sleep. So far today, the dog had spent time curled up on the sofa in the study, lounging in front of the fireplace, and sprawled across the freshly-made double bed in the guest room upstairs. He trotted out to the kitchen to get a drink of water from his dish, and then headed for the living room to sleep in front of the Christmas tree. He liked the smell of pine needles, and when he slept there, he always had good dreams about galloping around a beautiful forest. He had never understood why, when the weather got cold every year, his family would suddenly bring a tree into the house. But, having the tree around seemed to make everyone feel especially cheerful and jolly. So that made him happy, too.

He had lived with his family, the Callahans, for a very long time now. Two whole years! Two *wonderful* years. When he was a puppy, he had been a stray. He had lived in the streets, scavenging for food and shelter. More often than not, he had gone hungry. It was a very sad and lonely time for him.

But then, one day, he met a boy named Gregory. The dog had been sleeping near a big brick building. Every afternoon, children would come running outside, and play noisy games on the grass or in the snow. They always had so much fun that the dog liked watching them. Gregory, along with his sister, Patricia, and his friend Oscar, started bringing him food and water. Then the dog went to live with Gregory and Patricia, and their parents, Mr and Mrs Callahan. And, of course, Evelyn, the cat. He had been happy ever since. The dog loved his new family very much, and he and Gregory and

Patricia spent almost every waking moment together.

During the week, though, Gregory and Patricia would go off with their rucksacks full of books. Mrs Callahan also left in the mornings, with a big canvas briefcase. She was a physics teacher at the local high school, and would drop Gregory and Patricia off at the middle school on her way to work.

Mr Callahan was a writer. So, every day, he would stay at home, listen to music, and sit at his desk in the study. Sometimes he typed on a keyboard, but mostly he just sat there. The dog liked to sleep under the desk, and Mr Callahan would rest his feet on his back while he worked. Mr Callahan also liked to make lots of snacks, which he always shared. Sometimes, he would spend all day lying on the sofa and watching television and making phone calls. Today, Mr Callahan had prepared a thick salami sandwich on wholewheat toast for lunch, along with a bowl of crisps. The dog had enjoyed small tastes of each, but he preferred the salami. Evelyn did not like either, but she *did* stick her paw right into Mr Callahan's glass of milk. Mr Callahan was not thrilled about this, but he patted her and drank it, anyway.

Every weekday afternoon, the dog would start

waiting for Gregory and Patricia to come back from school. Starting around three-thirty, he would keep one ear cocked in the direction of the kitchen door. Lots of times lately, they hadn't got home until it was already dark outside! The dog would get very restless when this happened, and sometimes, he would pace around the kitchen endlessly until he heard the car in the drive.

Today seemed to be another one of those long days. As the afternoon wore on, the dog would only nap for a few minutes at a time. Then he would get up, and lift his paws on to the front windowsill to look outside. Sometimes, he whined softly. Where *were* they? What was taking so long?

Finding him at the window yet again, Mr Callahan patted him.

"Don't worry, Santa Paws," he said. "They'll be home as soon as practice is over. We have a couple of sports enthusiasts in the family now, that's all."

The dog wagged his tail when he heard his name. Although he had a lot of different nicknames, most of the people in town called him "Santa Paws". Gregory had originally named him Nicholas, but after months of hearing everyone else saying "Santa Paws", now the Callahans called him that, too. Patricia thought Santa Paws was a really stupid name – *beyond* not cool – but at this point, even she had given up and started using it routinely.

The dog was generally happy to answer to *any* name, but Santa Paws was his favourite. People always smiled when they said it, and he liked to see people smile. It seemed like a very merry name, indeed.

Finally, just after the sun went down, Santa Paws heard the crunch of car tyres on some frozen leaves in the drive. They were home! His family! Back where they belonged! The world was wonderful again! Yay!

The back door opened, bringing a rush of cold winter air into the kitchen. Mrs Callahan came in first, lugging a bag of groceries along with her briefcase. She usually had lots of homework papers to correct and lesson plans to prepare at night, so her briefcase was always full.

Gregory was next, also carrying a grocery bag in one arm. His rucksack was slung over his free shoulder. Gregory was twelve, and he was in the seventh grade this year. He was tall for his age, with dark brown hair and bright blue eyes. Underneath his ski jacket, he was still dressed in his basketball trainers, grey tracksuit trousers, a turtleneck with the sleeves cut off, and his favourite Phantom Menace T-shirt.

Patricia was the last one to come inside, weighed down by all of her hockey equipment. She looked a lot like Gregory, except that she always wore her hair in a bouncy ponytail. This year, the middle school had formed a junior-high girls' ice hockey team, and even though Patricia was very small and thin for her age, she had been one of the first people to sign up. Ice hockey "appealed to her lower instincts," was her explanation. "What does *that* mean?" Gregory would always ask. Patricia, who had never lacked confidence, would just sigh heavily and say, "If you have to ask, you'll never understand it." Gregory hadn't quite worked out an answer for that yet — but he knew an insult when he heard one. Privately, he kind of wondered if, on her birthday this year, instead of turning thirteen, Patricia hadn't actually turned *thirty-three*.

Overjoyed to have the entire family home safe and sound, Santa Paws began barking loudly. He jumped on each of them in turn, managing to knock Patricia down in the process. He weighed more than forty kilograms, and didn't always realize how strong he was.

"Maybe you should take your skates *off* before you come in the house," Gregory suggested.

Patricia just grinned wryly, although their mother glanced over to check her feet, looking alarmed. Mrs Callahan's expression relaxed when she saw that her daughter was actually wearing black cowboy boots.

"Did everyone have a good day?" Mr Callahan asked. "How was practice?"

"I'm really tired," Gregory said. "Oscar kept making me laugh, so Coach had us run about a million laps."

Mr Callahan winced, as he hated all forms of exercise. He had always said that playing chess was all the exertion he could handle. "How about you?" he asked Patricia. "Were you able to stay out of the penalty box?"

"Mostly," Patricia answered, and then she sighed. "They want me to be goalie, but I said no way."

"What's wrong with being the goalie?" Mrs Callahan asked, as she unpacked milk and orange juice from her grocery bag. "It's a very responsible position."

"Let people hit a really hard puck *at* me, and I'm not even allowed to duck?" Patricia shook her head. "No way. I have my teeth to think about."

"Besides, if you're stuck in the goal, you can't go around slamming people into the boards or anything," Gregory said.

"No," Patricia agreed, "and that's my favourite part."

Mr Callahan looked at his wife. "Remember when she was four years old, and *lived* for ballet class?"

"Dimly," Mrs Callahan said, with a grin.

As Patricia gathered up her hockey gear, Santa Paws grabbed one of her oversized gloves in his mouth and shook it playfully from side to side.

"Drop it, please," she said, holding out her hand. "Those are expensive."

Santa Paws was disappointed – he loved games! – but he let the glove slip back to the floor. "Drop it!" was one of the phrases like "Down!" and "No!" which he knew, but was always sad to hear.

"Good dog," she said.

That made Santa Paws cheer up. "Good dog" was a wonderful thing to hear. Almost as good as "Suppertime!" and "Want a Milk-Bone?"

When Mrs Callahan sent Gregory and Patricia upstairs to get cleaned up before dinner, Santa Paws followed them.

"Bags I shower first!" Patricia said.

"That's not fair – you *always* get the first one," Gregory protested.

Patricia shrugged. "That's because I'm older, and cleverer, and faster."

He wasn't sure about "cleverer," but she definitely had him on the other two. "Yeah, well – you're *short*," Gregory said.

Patricia laughed. "Is that the best you can do?"

Gregory nodded sheepishly. "Yeah, but only because I'm really tired. Otherwise, I could make fun of you for like, a whole hour. I'd be, you know, *merciless*."

"Oh," Patricia said, looking amused. "So, I should take pity on you, and give you the first shower?"

Gregory nodded again. "Yep. Also, because I'm younger, and slower, and your very favourite brother."

Patricia pushed up the sleeve of her Oceanport Mariners jersey to show him a large dark purple bruise on her elbow. "See what happened when I tackled Betsy Davenport? *I* should get the first shower."

Gregory promptly yanked his left tracksuit trouser leg up far enough to expose a huge puffy red scrape above his knee. "See what happened when *I* dived out of bounds for a loose ball?"

Confused by these demonstrations, Santa Paws sat down and lifted one paw. From force of habit, Gregory reached over to shake it, and Santa Paws wagged his tail. If they were going to play some kind of new game, he wanted to be included.

"Did it bleed?" Patricia asked, bending down to examine the injury.

"Of course," Gregory said proudly. "They even

used one of those instant ice packs and took me to the changing rooms to clean it."

"OK, you win." Patricia straightened up. "Don't use all the hot water."

"*If* you're lucky," Gregory said.

While Gregory showered, Patricia checked her e-mail. Then, while she was taking her turn, Gregory threw a tennis ball up and down the landing for Santa Paws. Santa Paws joyfully retrieved it each time, his paws scrabbling against the polished wooden floor. Sometimes he gave the ball back, but sometimes he was having so much fun that he kept it instead. Then Gregory would try to wrestle it free, with Santa Paws moving his head out of the way at *just* the right moment to avoid him. It was fun!

Once they had all trooped back downstairs for supper, Santa Paws alertly positioned himself right by the table. He never knew when someone might drop a piece of food, and he always liked to be ready for the possibility. Evelyn, the cat, was more subtle, and she just perched casually on a nearby worktop.

Mrs Callahan was serving the spaghetti when the telephone rang. Just as Mr Callahan was saying, "Wait, let the answerphone take it," Gregory was already racing across the room to answer it.

"Hello?" he said, and then saw his parents look at him sternly. "I mean, uh, this is the Callahan household." He listened for a minute, and then covered the receiver. "It's the police, Mum. They want to talk to you or Dad straight away."

As Mr Callahan's brother Steve was a member of the local police force, he hurried over. He immediately asked the officer on the other end if Steve was OK, and then looked relieved.

"Oh, good, you had me pretty worried there," Mr Callahan said into the phone. "So, what seems to be the problem?"

The rest of the family watched, as Mr Callahan listened, and nodded, and said things like "OK" and "I see." Finally, he nodded one last time, told the officer that they would come right away, and then hung up the phone.

"What is it?" Mrs Callahan asked uneasily. "Is something wrong?"

Mr Callahan nodded, his expression very serious. "It's an emergency," he said. "There's a missing child."

"Is it anyone we know?" Patricia asked.

Mr Callahan shook his head, already reaching for his jacket.

Gregory felt just as confused as his mother and sister looked. "So – I don't get it. Why did they call us?"

"Why else?" Mr Callahan said with a resigned shrug. "They need Santa Paws."

Chapter 2

Hearing his name, the dog pricked his ears up. Santa Paws was well known throughout the town of Oceanport – and all over New England – for being very good to have around during emergencies. In spite of himself, whenever there was trouble, he always ended up right in the middle of the situation. He had never *meant* to become a hero, but somehow, it had worked out that way. For some mysterious reason, he was especially good at helping people during the holiday season. He had performed so many rescues during the last two years that most of Oceanport thought he was a combination of Lassie and all 101 Dalmatians put together. A few of the more imaginative people in town might even have added ET to the list.

Santa Paws watched, baffled, as the entire family got up from the table *without even eating dinner*! What could they be thinking? It smelled so delicious!

In all the confusion, Evelyn sneaked on to the table and stole a meatball. The dog hoped she might share it, but she just hissed at him and carried her treasure off to the living room to eat in privacy. He was afraid to follow her, in case she might scratch him.

"We don't *all* need to go," Mr Callahan said, as he reached for the car keys. "Why don't you kids wait here, and—"

"We want to help!" Gregory protested.

"We *know* we can help," Patricia said confidently. She zipped up her warmest jacket, and put on her gloves and New England Patriots cap.

Mr and Mrs Callahan looked at each other.

"The longer we stand here discussing it, the longer that poor child is out there alone in the cold," Mrs Callahan said.

Mr Callahan nodded, and motioned for everyone to come along. His wife yanked him back, and pointed at his feet. Mr Callahan blushed, as he was wearing Pink Panther slippers. Because he worked at home, he often forgot to change into proper clothes before he went outside.

"I'll start the car," Mrs Callahan said, "while you get your boots."

It wasn't quite cold enough to snow, but an icy rain was falling and they would certainly all *need* their boots out there.

Santa Paws still couldn't work out why nobody wanted to eat supper, but he barked happily when he saw Gregory holding his lead. He loved riding in cars, and maybe they were going on a special adventure! He was always ready for that!

On the drive over, Mr Callahan explained the whole story. A family named the Jensens, who lived near the edge of town, had a two–year–old boy, Robert. No one was quite sure how, but Robert had wandered away a couple of hours earlier. His family had searched their house and garden frantically, and then called the police. The police organized search parties immediately, but there was no sign of Robert anywhere. Most of the nearby neighbours had volunteered to help, with no success. Now it was dark, and getting cold enough outside so that everyone was starting to panic. If they didn't find him soon, it might be too late!

The Jensens' house was easy to find, because there were police cars and other emergency service vehicles parked all over the place. There were even vans from the local television stations, reporting live from the scene. When the Callahans pulled up, a very young female officer came over to stop them.

"I'm sorry, ma'am," she said politely. "But this area is restricted right now. You'll need to take a different route."

"We were asked to come," Mrs Callahan said. "We have Santa Paws with us."

"Oh!" Now the officer looked very respectful. "Right this way. You'll need to report to Sergeant Callahan."

Mr Callahan couldn't help grinning, as Sergeant Callahan was, of course, his little brother Steve. While recuperating from some severe injuries, Steve had had plenty of time to study for the sergeant's exam the previous spring. His score was the highest in the whole department, so he had been promoted, even though he was still mostly on desk duty. Steve had actually been injured the Christmas before, when his private plane crashed in the mountains. All these months later, the hip he had broken was still bothering him. Patricia, Gregory and Santa Paws had been flying with him that day, and – well, they still all felt very grateful to have survived.

None of them liked planes much any more, either.

The Callahans and Santa Paws followed the female police officer down the street and across the Jensens' lawn. The entire atmosphere was tense and chaotic. The Jensens' house was surrounded by woods on three sides, so there were plenty of dangerous places for a tiny child to get lost. People were shouting orders and questions, and torchlight beams bobbed up and down through the trees as search parties worked desperately to find Robert.

"Hi, Uncle Steve!" Gregory said, as they walked up to the command post.

Uncle Steve was leaning on his stick and looked very tired, but he turned to smile at them. "Hi, guys," he said. "Thanks for getting here so quickly."

An officer wearing a uniform from one of the neighbouring towns came over, looking discouraged. "Nothing in Sector Four. Sorry."

Uncle Steve sighed and marked the area off on a grid map. "OK. Give your people a few minutes to have some coffee and warm up, and then have them double-check Sector Seven."

The officer nodded, and left.

Uncle Steve turned his attention back to his family. "We're not getting anywhere," he said in a low voice. "And no one's even sure if the kid had a sweater on, let alone a jacket. We wanted to use dogs straight away, but the nearest SAR team is still on a job out in the Berkshires right now. We sent for one of the Boston K-9 Units, but they're taking for ever to get here. I'm sorry to drag you all out like this, but I thought Santa Paws could probably help."

"SAR?" Gregory whispered to Patricia. He had never heard those initials before, and wasn't sure what they meant.

"Search and Rescue," she whispered back.

He nodded. Since he was *almost* sure that "K-9" was slang for "Canine", he decided not to ask about that one.

A burly man in a Massachusetts State Police uniform came lumbering over when he saw Santa Paws.

"Is this the hotshot dog?" he asked dubiously. "Well, let's get started." He stretched out his hand and indicated for Gregory to give him the lead.

Santa Paws didn't like the idea of going off with a complete stranger, so he sat down firmly.

"It's OK, boy," Gregory said, patting him.

Santa Paws wagged his tail briefly, but still didn't budge.

Gregory looked tentatively at the state trooper. "I, um, don't think he'll obey someone he doesn't know, sir."

The trooper, whose last name was Yeager, looked impatient. "Fine. Whatever." He turned to Steve. "We'll just have to wait for the K-9 team, then."

"But he'll go with *us*," Gregory assured him. "He's really good at finding things."

Trooper Yeager frowned at Uncle Steve. "The last thing we need is some kids and an amateur dog mucking up our search, Callahan."

"With all due respect, sir," Uncle Steve said, his voice both polite and testy, "this actually falls within my jurisdiction, and I'm giving the OK." He turned to a nearby Oceanport paramedic. "Ask one of the Jensens to come over here, please."

A very pale woman in her early thirties was led to the command post by the paramedic. Her hands were trembling badly and it was easy to see that she had been crying. The Callahans knew without asking that she must be Robert's mother. When she saw Santa Paws, her face fell.

"But – I thought he'd be a purebred," she said, her voice shaking. "Are you sure this is really Santa Paws? This dog looks like a *house pet*."

Gregory and Patricia both felt insulted, as they thought Santa Paws was beautiful. Dashing, even. He was mostly Alsatian, with some collie mixed in, and had thick brown fur, with black highlights on his face and tail. The American Kennel Club would be *lucky* to have such a fine dog in their organization.

"We're very sorry about your son, ma'am," Patricia said crisply, before anyone else could speak. "Could you please get us some clothes Robert wore recently, from his laundry basket, maybe? Whatever you think will have the strongest scent."

Mrs Jensen seemed a little startled that a girl seemed to be taking charge of the situation – but no one who knew Patricia was ever surprised by things like that. She had always told people that she wanted to be a police officer, or a Supreme Court Justice – or the President of the United States, when she grew up. Gregory, personally, had his money on President. Unless, of course, the United States switched to a monarchy, and then he knew Patricia would insist upon being the *Queen*.

"Yes, of course," Mrs Jensen said, without arguing. "I'll be back in a minute."

Trooper Yeager – who had never met Patricia – put his hands on his hips. "Would you mind telling this kid we can run our own operation, Sergeant?"

"Actually, no," Uncle Steve said mildly. "Instead of fighting, let's just try to find Robert, OK?"

"Well, I don't like it," Trooper Yeager said. "I don't want some *kid*—"

Mrs Callahan, who had something of a temper herself, stepped forward. "This 'kid' is my daughter, mister, and I'd appreciate it if you didn't—"

"Here it is, here it is!" Mrs Jensen said, rushing over with a tiny red shirt.

Everyone at the command post smiled tensely at her, and there seemed to be a silent agreement not to argue in front of the little boy's mother. Santa Paws just sat next to Gregory, completely perplexed. He could tell that everyone around him was very upset, but he wasn't sure what was going on.

"Thank you, ma'am," Patricia said, and handed the shirt to Gregory. "Don't worry about a thing. Santa Paws is *really* clever."

Since they fully agreed with that, her parents and Uncle Steve nodded.

Gregory held the shirt up to his dog's nose. "Smell that, OK, boy?"

Santa Paws sniffed cooperatively. He could smell a little boy, some slightly spoiled milk, and a faint odour of strained spinach. He sniffed again, and then wagged his tail at Gregory.

"Good dog!" Gregory praised him. "Now, find the boy!"

Santa Paws sat down again, puzzled. Find. He knew the word "find". He just wasn't sure *what* they wanted him to find.

"Oh, it's no use," Mrs Jensen said, near tears. "We'll have to wait for the real dogs to come."

After the plane crash, Gregory had told Santa Paws to "find the car" – and he had led them several kilometres across the White Mountains, through a blizzard, until they got to a motorway. So he was sure that his dog could find anything, as long as he understood what they were asking.

Gregory held the shirt up to his nose again. "Come on, Santa Paws, you can do it!"

The dog sniffed for a long time, and then sniffed the air again. There were so many people around, plus exhaust fumes from the cars, that it was hard to separate all of the different scents from one another. But now he had it! He jumped to his feet, and led them confidently towards the house.

"He's not there!" Mrs Jensen groaned. "We've all searched over and over."

"Let's just trust the dog, ma'am," Uncle Steve said, very calm. "His sense of smell is much better than ours."

Santa Paws led them straight to the house, swiped his paw across the back door, and then sat down. Mrs Jensen obviously thought this was a waste of time, but she opened the door. Santa Paws sniffed the air and headed straight for the pedal bin in the corner of the kitchen. He banged his paw against the lid, and sat down again, wagging his tail. This search didn't make any sense, but he wanted to make them all happy.

Gregory looked more closely at the shirt in the bright indoor light, and saw the milk and food stains. He opened the pedal bin, and lifted out an empty milk carton, and a used polystyrene plate covered with the remains of a meal.

"Oh, it's useless," Mrs Jensen said, crying. "That's only what Robert had for lunch. This is just a waste of time."

"I agree," Trooper Yeager said grimly. "This may be your jurisdiction, Callahan, but—"

"Did Robert spill any on his shirt?" Patricia asked.

Mrs Jensen stared at her, and then stopped crying for a minute. "Actually, he *did*. Is that what your dog smelled?"

Gregory nodded. "He's not sure what we want him to find. Could you bring us some more clothes, so he'll know that we're looking for *Robert*, not food?"

For the first time, there was some hope in Mrs Jensen's expression. She hurried into the laundry room and came out with more clothes. Gregory held each piece of clothing in turn up to his dog's nose.

"Find the boy, Santa Paws!" he said. "Find the little boy!"

The dog cocked his head.

"*Fetch* the little boy," Patricia said. "We want you to fetch the little boy for us."

The dog bounded to his feet. He *definitely* knew the word "fetch"! He ran over to the door, and barked twice. Once he was outside, he began sniffing around the steps and the drive. There were traces of the very same human scent all over the garden, but some were more recent than others. He sniffed the ground, and then the air, trying to find the freshest one. The icy rain was washing away some of the smells – and also falling in his eyes – but he just kept sniffing. There it was, heading away from the house, only a couple of hours old! He barked and started along the trail.

A bright light beamed across the snow from the street, near one of the television vans. Apparently, a cameraperson was trying to film the search. Uncle Steve quickly sent two officers over to order the cameras turned off for the time being. He didn't want anything to distract Santa Paws right now.

The dog followed the trail as closely as he could, ignoring all of the chaos around him. It was strange, because the scent went back and forth and around in circles, with no logical pattern. But Santa Paws doggedly just kept following his nose.

"What kind of crazy path is *that*?" Trooper Yeager grumbled.

"Have you ever seen a two–year–old run around before?" Mrs Callahan asked.

Trooper Yeager thought about that, and then closed his mouth.

The trail started leading downhill, towards the thickest part of the woods. Because of the rain, everyone was slipping and sliding on the icy grass. Since he had trouble moving quickly on his stick, and also had to run the search, Uncle Steve limped back to the command post. Mrs Jensen had gone to get her husband, who was off searching in another sector.

Santa Paws veered back and forth, snuffling the ground every so often, but mostly keeping his nose in the air as he tracked the scent. He trotted into the forest, winding between trees in a crooked and unpredictable route.

"We've searched this whole area already," one of the nearby police officers said softly. "It's clean."

"Shhh," someone else hissed. "The dog seems to know what he's doing."

Santa Paws plunged forward through the undergrowth, and then he paused. He sniffed the air, turning his head from side to side. Then he pushed on deeper into the woods.

Ahead, there was a sound of water rushing. He followed the scent in that same direction, and soon came across a stream with a fairly strong current. He put his nose to the ground at the water's edge and inhaled deeply. The scent seemed to stop at the stream. Santa Paws sat down for a minute, not sure why he had lost the trail. How could it be there one second, and gone the next?

Gregory patted his head. "Come on, pal, you can do it. Find Robert!"

"If that poor little boy fell in the water, who knows how far it could have carried him downstream," Trooper Yeager said, his eyes dark with concern. "Tell the dog to hurry."

Just then, Santa Paws got up, and began to run back and forth along the side of the stream. He explored each direction, but was still stumped.

The little boy's scent had disappeared!

Chapter 3

Now Trooper Yeager took charge. "All right, we don't have a minute to lose." He flicked on his walkie-talkie. "I want all the units in Sectors One to Three to assemble near the stream. We need some more manpower down here."

Suddenly, the dog's ears went up. Santa Paws turned his head to one side, and then jumped into the water. It was very cold, but he didn't even flinch as he started splashing his way downstream. He had picked up the scent again!

Gregory went into the water right after him, yelping when the freezing liquid bit into his legs. Patricia was only a couple of steps behind them. There were rocks under the water, and they both had a hard time keeping their balance. Their parents and all of the officers and volunteers followed closely.

Santa Paws stopped about three metres away, and stuck his head into something below the overhanging bank. Then he turned towards Gregory and Patricia, and barked triumphantly.

"He's found him, wow!" Gregory said. "What a good dog!"

Santa Paws barked, and wagged his tail as hard as he could. He was always so happy when they called him a good dog!

"Wait a minute," Mrs Callahan called, as she and the others tried to catch up. "Why don't you two stay there, and let your father and me go first."

Gregory was already crouching down underneath the bank. In the dim light from the torches upstream, he could see the outline of a drainage pipe. The pipe was less than fifty centimetres wide – too small for a normal person to fit through. But by squinting his eyes, he could just make out the shape of a small figure lying down about three metres inside. The sight horrified him so much that he leaped backwards and ended up sitting in the water.

"Oh, no, we're too late," he gasped. "He's not moving!"

Patricia gulped, but pushed past him to see for herself. She was carrying a small penlight, which she flashed into the pipe. Then, she smiled.

"Relax, Greg," she said. "It's called *sleeping*."

Gregory picked himself up, not even noticing that he had got completely soaked. "Are you sure? Is he OK?"

Patricia nodded. "Absolutely. I can see him breathing."

More people were crowding around now, and inside the pipe Robert woke up when he heard the commotion. He started crying when he saw all the unfamiliar faces, and then he retreated further into the pipe. Everyone seemed to be talking at once, which must have confused the little boy even more.

"Give us some room, kids, OK?" one of the Oceanport police officers asked. "We have to get him out of there."

Gregory and Patricia politely stepped aside. Santa Paws stood in between them, panting a little, but still wagging his tail.

"Good boy," Gregory said, resting his gloved hand on his dog's head. "You're very, *very* good."

Santa Paws wagged his tail. Yay! Gregory thought he was good!

"You're very, very *clever*," Patricia said, also patting him.

And Patricia thought he was clever! "Clever" was a good word, too!

"Come on, Robert," the Oceanport officer was saying in a soothing voice, as he extended one arm into the pipe. "Time to go home and see Mummy and Daddy."

Robert cried, and crawled further away, almost out of sight.

One of the paramedics tried next, but she didn't have any luck, either. "He's too far in there," she said, standing up in the creek. "We're going to need the rescue equipment.

The diameter of the pipe was tiny, but –

"Maybe I can fit inside," Gregory offered shyly.

"It's worth a shot," the paramedic said, and gave him a boost up.

Gregory did his best, but his shoulders were just too wide for him to be able to squeeze through. If he managed to climb in at all, he would get stuck immediately.

"All right," Trooper Yeager said from his position in the middle of the stream. "Let's get his parents down here, have them coax him out. Find out what sectors they're in. Come on, make it snappy!"

A couple of officers hurried off to find ropes and anything else they might need, while two others went to find the Jensens. The total search area was very large, and they could be almost *anywhere*.

Patricia watched all of the excitement for a minute, and then let out her breath. "I'm a lot thinner than you are," she said to Gregory.

"Yeah," he conceded, "but you get scared in small places."

Patricia nodded, but shrugged off her jacket and handed it to him. She *hated* small places. To make sure she would be as slender as possible, she took off her sweater and turtleneck, too. That left her standing in the freezing rain in nothing but a T-shirt, as well as her jeans and walking boots, and she started shivering.

"Patricia, put your jacket right back on," Mrs Callahan said sharply. "The rescue squad will be able to get him out. They're trained for this."

Patricia looked at her. "Would you want them to come digging after one of *us* with ropes and chainsaws and all? If you could avoid it? And would you want to *wait* for all of that, if you didn't have to?"

Her mother hesitated just long enough for Patricia to know she had won the argument. So Patricia went over and tapped Trooper Yeager on the arm.

He glanced down, looking annoyed, as he was passing on some official communications over his walkie-talkie. "Look, thanks, kid, your dog did a great job. But, we're really busy now, OK?"

"I can fit in there," Patricia said. "My brother's bigger than I am."

Trooper Yeager started to disagree, but then looked her over more carefully. "You know what, kid, you're right. You probably *can*." He glanced at Mr and Mrs Callahan. "It OK with you if we give it a go?"

Mr and Mrs Callahan nodded reluctantly.

"Why don't we wait for the ropes, at least," Mr Callahan said. "And then—"

"Don't worry, Dad, I can fit," Patricia said, sounding very confident. "It'll only take a minute."

One of the paramedics taped a small torch to Patricia's forearm, so that she would be able to see where she was going, but still have her hands free. Then Patricia bent down and peered inside the tiny pipe.

"Whoa," she said, her voice trembling a little. "That's really small!"

"Patricia—" Her father started, his voice worried.

But before she could let herself change her mind, Patricia took another deep breath and started crawling into the pipe. It might make more sense to wait for the rescue crew – but, well, she had never exactly been a patient person.

There wasn't much room to spare, and she could only just guide herself forward. Her shoulders and hips were jammed against the cold cement on either side, but she forced herself not to think about how confined she was. Once she had gone about three metres, she angled her arm so the torch wouldn't shine straight in Robert's eyes. The little boy was so surprised to see someone coming in after him that he had stopped crying.

"Babysitter?" he asked, his voice sounding weak from being outside in the cold so long. His nose was running pretty badly, too.

The sides of the pipe seemed to be pressing even more tightly around her, and for a second, Patricia was afraid she wouldn't be able to breathe. But she forced a smile, so that Robert wouldn't be scared. Or, at any rate, not as scared as *she* was.

"Y-yeah, sometimes I'm a babysitter," she said. "Your mummy and daddy are waiting outside." She *hoped*. "Want to take my hand, so we can go and see them?"

Robert's face lit up. "Mummy and Daddy?!"

"Robert?" a woman's voice called, her voice echoing through the pipe. To Patricia's relief, it sounded like Mrs Jensen. "Bobby, please come here!"

"Mummy!" Robert said with a big smile. He

laughed, and clapped his hands together a few times. "Where's Mummy?"

"She's right outside." Patricia reached out again. "Take my hand, OK? Then we can go and see your mummy." Using her foot for leverage, she pushed herself forward a few more centimetres, and Robert crawled over to meet her. His hand was terribly cold, and she could see that his teeth were chattering. "OK, good," she said, making sure her voice sounded hearty. "Come on."

It was slow going, but she gradually made her way backwards towards the opening of the pipe, clutching Robert's hand the entire time. If he pulled away, she might have to stay in here even longer! Then her feet hit a pile of old leaves, and she lost her momentum. Her legs kept slipping, and she couldn't get her free hand in position to help push them past the leaves. As far as she could tell, they were trapped!

"Dad, help!" she shouted, trying not to panic. "Dad! I think I'm stuck."

"It's OK, Patricia, we're going to get you out," Mr Callahan said from the end of the pipe.

She could tell that he was reaching for them, but they were still too far inside.

"Patricia, you just hang on, OK?" he said. "They're coming with the ropes right now."

Patricia swallowed, suddenly feeling as though

the pipe was squeezing against her with so much force that it was compressing her lungs. This maybe hadn't been a very good plan, after all. It was hard to get her breath, and she closed her eyes, forcing herself to count to ten. Twenty. Thirty. Robert must have sensed her fear, because he started crying again.

"Want to go *home*," he sobbed. "Want to go home *now*."

"You and me both," Patricia said shakily, doing her best to smile at him. She kicked at the leaves as hard as she could, but now wasn't sure if she could go forward *or* backwards. Where were the ropes? What was taking so long? Not that she was on the verge of hysteria or anything – but they really did seem to be stuck. Helpless. *Trapped*.

Could she stand it in here for another few minutes? Another few *seconds*? Forget the rescue squad – it was time to call in the cavalry. "Santa Paws!" she yelled. "Help!"

She heard him bark, and then he leaped out of the stream and squirmed inside the narrow space. It seemed impossible for such a big dog to be able to fit into the pipe, but he stubbornly wormed his way towards them. Then he grabbed her boot with his teeth and tugged her a few centimetres closer to safety, through the musty leaves.

"Good boy," Patricia said, some of her panic

fading. If anyone could get her out of here, Santa Paws could. "You can do it, boy!"

Santa Paws kept pulling, until her boot came right off. He seemed surprised, but then dropped it and began wriggling towards her again. This time, he dug his teeth into her jeans leg and tugged with all of his might. As she hung on to Robert, Santa Paws dragged both of them all the way to the pipe's opening before scrambling free. He landed in the stream with a big splash, and barked a few times.

Working together, Mr Callahan and Trooper Yeager carefully eased Patricia and Robert the rest of the way out. Mrs Jensen quickly grabbed her son into a tight hug, while she cried and tried to thank everyone at once. Just then, Mr Jensen, who had been off searching in the furthest sector, came running towards them. He was also crying, and hugged his wife and son as hard as he could.

"Thank you so much," Mrs Jensen said over and over. "Thank you, you're all so wonderful! Thank you!"

Once again, Santa Paws had saved the day!

Chapter 4

Everyone took turns shaking hands, patting Santa Paws, and congratulating one another. The icy rain was now just plain sleet, but no one even noticed. With Robert alive and well – and back where he belonged, the cold winter storm didn't seem very important. As soon as he got a chance, Santa Paws retrieved Patricia's sopping wet boot from where it had fallen in the creek and brought it to her.

"*You* are a really good dog," she said, and gave him a big hug. She was feeling much better now that she was outside – and her mother had helped her put her sweater and coat back on. If Robert ever got lost again, she hoped that he would pick a much *larger* tunnel next time.

"He's a *great* dog," Gregory agreed.

"For a house pet," Patricia said, and they both laughed quietly.

Santa Paws let his tail wave merrily. The cheerful mood of celebration surrounding them was contagious. It was almost like being at a party!

There were glaring camera lights everywhere, and lots of noise. Some of the television news crews had come down to film the joyful reunion of parents and toddler. The woods and stream were so crowded that it made everything seem that much more hectic and confusing. Although Robert seemed to be fine, his parents and the paramedics were taking him to a waiting ambulance. He would be whisked off to the hospital for a full check-up, just to make sure that he had survived his ordeal without any problems.

The Callahans and Santa Paws waded out of the water and climbed up the slippery slope through the woods. Now that the command post was being dismantled, Uncle Steve came to meet them. He was moving cautiously on his stick, but he had a huge grin on his face.

"Pretty outstanding work," he said cheerfully. "Any of you want to be deputized?"

Patricia thought about that. "Would we be given full arrest powers, and everything?"

"Truth is, all *I* really want is some supper," Gregory said.

Now Patricia realized that she was hungry, too. "Hey, that's right! We never had dinner!"

Both of their parents looked guilty. By now, their long-forgotten spaghetti would be too cold and stale to eat.

"Is it OK if we go home?" Mr Callahan asked his little brother. "Make them some dinner?"

"Absolutely," Uncle Steve said. "If we're lucky, you can escape the press, too."

But, he had spoken too soon. Since the ambulance holding the Jensens was pulling away now, most of the reporters swarmed over to shout questions at the Callahans. In the meantime, the cameras were all focusing on Santa Paws. This turned out to be rather poor timing, since he had just stopped to lift his leg against a tree.

"A great film moment," Patricia muttered to Gregory, and they both laughed.

"What's it like to own a hero dog?" one reporter asked.

"Can you tell us how he knew where to find the little boy?" another one wanted to know.

"Is it true that he dived into a well, and saved the Jensen boy from drowning?" a third chimed in.

Mrs Callahan raised her hands for silence. "I'm sorry," she said, with the particularly authoritative and dismissive tone that only platoon sergeants – and longtime teachers – know how to use effectively. Nuns can sometimes do it, too. "But right now, we need to get our children home, and fed, and into some dry clothes. I'm sure Sergeant Callahan will be happy to answer any questions you have."

Uncle Steven grinned wryly. "Oh, yeah. Delighted." He summoned a few Oceanport officers over. "Clear a path, and escort my brother and his family to their car, OK?"

"Could we at least interview the *dog*?" one particularly persistent reporter asked plaintively.

Gregory leaned over to Patricia. "His – how you say in English? – verbal skills are not so good, no?"

Patricia gave him an affectionate shove. "You're an idiot, Greg, you know that?"

He nodded. "Well, yeah – since you tell me all the time."

Santa Paws let out a happy bark, and nudged Gregory's leg with his muzzle. Romping was one of his favourite ways to spend time. If they wrestled here, they would be able to get nice and muddy, too!

"Could he just *pose* for a minute?" a cameraman asked.

Mr Callahan rolled his eyes, but told Santa Paws to sit.

Santa Paws promptly sat down, as the cameras

swung in his direction. He was blinded by all of the lights, and instinctively raised one paw. The reporters were thrilled, since it was the sort of thing Lassie would have done. His coat was still soaked from running around in the stream, and he stood up to shake off as much of the water as he could. Then he sneezed, looked surprised, and sneezed again. The reporters found this less exciting, but kept filming anyway.

Gregory, Patricia and their mother were already in the car by now. Santa Paws saw the open door and raced over to leap inside. It was too cold out in the sleet! Mr Callahan quickly got into the driver's seat and started the car.

As they drove away, Gregory and Patricia watched the press turn around and move to surround Uncle Steve, instead. He seemed as blinded by the lights as Santa Paws had been.

"You know, tonight was a really weird night," Patricia said thoughtfully. "I mean, even weirder than usual."

Since it was hard to disagree with that, everyone else in the car nodded.

"Hey! Can we get pizzas?" Gregory asked.

"Of course," Mr Callahan said. "You can have anything you want. I'll drop you all off at home, and then I'll go out again. Do you want some ice cream, too?"

Gregory and Patricia nodded enthusiastically. They were very fond of ice cream.

Since they were obviously all happy, Santa Paws thumped his tail against the backseat. Their rainy, outdoor walk in the woods tonight had been much too congested and noisy for his taste, but he had still had a good time. He *liked* all of the adventures he and the Callahans had together, even if he didn't always understand what was going on. As far as he was concerned, he had the best family anywhere. And maybe there would even be some meatballs left when they got home! Yay!

"How about you, Santa Paws?" Mr Callahan asked, glancing at him in the rearview mirror. "Would you like an *extra*-large box of Milk-Bones?"

The dog's ears shot up, and his tail wagged even harder. Mr Callahan had just said his favourite word in the whole world.

Milk-Bones!

Little Robert Jensen's dramatic rescue was the lead story on all of the local news broadcasts that night. Each used a different tag line, from "Hero Dog!" to "Santa Paws Saves the Day!" to "North Shore Nail-biter". One channel even played a few bars from the "Lassie" theme when they flashed Santa Paws' picture across the screen. Patricia was appalled by how wet and bedraggled she appeared on camera, which Gregory found very entertaining. His filmed image was just as dishevelled, but he was pleased, because he thought it kind of made him look like an action hero. Mr and Mrs Callahan just kept shaking their heads, although they laughed when they watched Uncle Steve unenthusiastically reading the police department's official statement aloud. Uncle Steve liked *police work*, not public relations.

Throughout all of this, Santa Paws just sprawled on the rug in front of the fireplace and chewed energetically on the rawhide bone Mr Callahan had brought home as a special prize for him. It was fun! His coat was damp, because straight after Patricia and Gregory had had their baths, Mrs Callahan had given him one, too. But the fire in the fireplace was so nice and hot that it was helping him dry off. He wasn't cold at all any more. And soon, it would be time for everyone to go upstairs to sleep. That would be fun, too!

The next day was Saturday, and it was exactly a week before Christmas. Mrs Callahan still had a little bit of shopping left to do, and she decided to go to the mall. Patricia, Gregory and Santa Paws piled into the car with her. They weren't planning to be gone very long, so Mrs Callahan thought it would be just fine to bring Santa Paws along. It also wasn't very cold, so he would be perfectly comfortable waiting in the car. Mr Callahan always said the mall made him too anxious, so he was staying at home to listen to Frank Sinatra CDs and work on his new novel. In exactly that order, the rest of them suspected.

As they drove through the streets of Oceanport, almost everyone they passed waved and shouted things like "Way to go, Santa Paws!". The people in cars all beeped their horns, too. The entire town must have seen the news the night before, or else read the morning edition of the local newspaper. Now they wanted to congratulate their local celebrity. Santa Paws wasn't sure why the people were being so friendly, but it made him feel good.

Patricia slouched down in the front seat, and pulled her Red Sox cap over her eyes. She was still self-conscious about how silly she had looked on television. "I wish this could all be a little more low profile," she grumbled.

Gregory grinned, and slung his arm around his dog. "Hey, it's tough living with a superstar."

Santa Paws leaned over to lick his face, and then turned to look out of the window some more. For him, the best part about riding in cars was watching all of the scenery speed by.

The mall was very crowded, and they had to park in one of the furthest car parks.

"Are you sure you can walk this far," Gregory teased his sister, "or should we send a special cart back for you?"

"Hey, when it comes to being a big baby, *you're* the one who—" Patricia began.

"No wrangling," Mrs Callahan said instantly. "It's going to be hectic enough in there without the two of you fighting the whole time."

Patricia looked innocent. "Us? Fight?"

"Never," Gregory agreed.

"That's more like it," their mother said. "Now, come on. The sooner we go in there, the sooner we'll be finished."

Gregory lowered each of the back windows halfway, and reached through the closest opening to pat Santa Paws on the head. "Be a good dog, boy. Guard the car!"

Santa Paws barked once, and wagged his tail. Then he settled against the back seat to wait for them to come back. He hoped that it wouldn't take too long.

Once they were out of sight, he sneaked up into the front seat. The view was much better from there. He lounged on the driver's side, resting his paw on the steering wheel for balance.

A young man walking by gasped. "Look at that!" he said to his girlfriend. "He can even *drive*."

"Wow," the girl said, and shook her head with

admiration. Was there *anything* the magical Santa Paws couldn't do? He had to be the cleverest dog who had ever existed.

Santa Paws sat in the driver's seat for what seemed like a very long time. Then he decided he needed some fresh air, and he vaulted into the back again to stick his nose out of the window. For variety, he jumped over into the boot space, too. But the roof of the car was too low for him to be able to stand up comfortably, so he returned to the back seat. Now what?

Oh, right. Fresh air. He stuck his nose out as far as he could, and breathed deeply. Because they were in a car park, he mostly just smelled petrol, and exhaust fumes, and other car smells. There was a Burger King nearby, and if he concentrated, he could pick out the odours of grease, chips and hamburgers. Well, that was more like it!

He sniffed and sniffed, until he got tired. Then he sat down to decide what to do next. Should he jump back in the front? No, he had already *done* that. Had he had a nap yet? He thought hard, but he couldn't remember. Besides, he wasn't *that* tired. He yawned a few times, just in case, but he was still wide awake. In fact, he was bored! Would the Callahans *ever* come back? This was *awful*.

Feeling very unhappy, Santa Paws flung himself down on to the seat and lay there miserably for a minute. He was so bored, and so lonely. How long had they been gone? It felt like hours. Years, even. He sighed loudly, and even whimpered once. He just felt horrible being alone like this. But, wait – he smelled a tennis ball! Where was it? He snuffled around the floor of the car until he located his quarry buried under the front seat on the passenger's side. It was jammed between an old box of Kleenex and a first aid kit. There were some maps blocking his way, too.

Using his front paw, he managed to dig the ball out. The faded yellow cover was battered, and it smelled faintly of the sea. Maybe he and Gregory had been playing catch at the beach one time? It was hard to remember. Anyway, now he had a ball. He would *never* be bored now!

He shook his head from side to side, growling playfully, and pretending to defeat the ball in an epic battle. And – he won! The ball was completely at his mercy. What a good game! Now he stretched across the back seat, and dropped the ball between his front paws so he could admire it. The cover tasted too salty when he chewed it, so he let the ball fall from his mouth and land in front of him again. *This* was a good game, too!

So he spent a while picking the ball up, dropping it, and then repeating the cycle. Finally the ball bounced away and rolled under the front seat again. Santa Paws tried to retrieve it, but this time, the ball was too far underneath for him to reach. It was gone! No more ball! No more *fun*. Would Gregory come back and find it for him? The dog barked frantically, but he couldn't see his family, or even smell them.

He slumped down, feeling very sorry for himself. He was even too unhappy to take a nap. If *only* they would come back. He wanted his ball, he wanted a snack, and he wanted his family. Why were they taking so long?

Except that he actually *was* feeling a little sleepy. And his back itched. The itch was in one of the difficult spots to reach, and he had to twist his body in several directions before he could extend his paw to scratch just the right spot. *Ahhh.* Yes. While he was at it, he scratched up behind his left ear, too.

Now he felt *much* more comfortable. It was time for a little nap. He yawned widely, turned around three times on the seat, and plopped down. But the metal edge of a seatbelt buckle was pressing right against his ribs. Ow! So, he got up, repeated his three turns, and made sure he landed in a different spot this time.

Perfect! Now he could enjoy a nice, peaceful rest.

Santa Paws was sleeping soundly, when he

suddenly sensed that something was wrong. He opened his eyes, not sure what had woken him up. Voices. Unfamiliar, coarse voices. There were people right by the car! *Strangers!*

His eyes flew open, and he leaped to his feet. Just as he started barking, a metal crowbar smashed against the window. The glass broke and showered all over him. These were bad, bad people. They were hurting the car! Just as he lunged towards them to defend the car, the man in front shoved a thick wet cloth at him. The cloth was dripping with some sort of liquid and it smelled just terrible. His nose was filled with a sharp, unpleasant scent, like medicine at the vet's surgery.

For some reason, the overpowering smell made him feel very dizzy. He tried to bark and growl, but he could feel his legs crumpling. What was happening? Why did he feel so sick? The people – it was two mean-looking men – were opening the door now and reaching for him. Santa Paws gathered all of his strength to try and attack them, but his muscles didn't want to work. The scent on the cloth was just too strong, and all of a sudden, he fainted.

"OK, good," one of the men said. "He won't give us any trouble now."

"We'd better hurry, Chuck," the other man said.

"Yeah, yeah, yeah," the first one, Chuck, answered. "Just get in the van and keep the engine running." The men were brothers, and their names were Chuck and Eddie Hawthorne. Chuck was the older of the two, but Eddie was both fatter – and meaner.

While Eddie got into the old grey van next to the car, Chuck reached into his jacket pocket. He took out a heavy leather muzzle and buckled it around the dog's nose and head. This was one dog who wouldn't try biting *him* again! Then, he unfastened Santa Paws' collar and cruelly let it fall on to the back seat.

"Hurry up!" Eddie yelled. "Before someone comes!"

Chuck lifted up the unconscious dog, grunting with the effort. This stupid dog was *heavy*. But he was worth a lot of money, and he and Eddie were going to get rich from this caper! The Hawthornes had grown up in a nearby town, and they had been in trouble with the law on and off for years. Mostly they robbed and burgled, although sometimes they liked to pass dud cheques and do forgery, too. This time they had been hired to steal the famous dog, Santa Paws, by a rich, greedy man down in New Jersey who was going to buy the dog and keep him as part of his collection of exotic animals. Fifty thousand dollars! Chuck and Eddie had never even seen money like that, and in a few hours, it would be theirs! For the two thieves, it was going to be a very profitable Christmas!

Chuck hauled the dog over to the van and dumped him inside. Then he climbed in after him, and slammed the door.

"Let's scram!" he ordered.

Eddie put his foot on the accelerator, and the van squealed across the car park. The cement was icy, and they skidded a little, but Eddie got the van under control. There was lots of traffic, and it made Eddie very impatient to have to wait in a queue. He muttered, and grumbled, and tapped on the steering wheel. Then he cut up two cars and steered the van away from the mall, going the wrong way through the entrance, instead of using the exit. He almost hit a minivan crowded with holiday shoppers, but he just laughed and drove faster. Along with their many other faults, the Hawthorne boys were really bad drivers, too. Soon, they would be on the motorway and heading for New Jersey.

They had just pulled off the best robbery of their lives!

Chapter 5

When they had finally finished their shopping, the Callahans came outside, loaded down with bags. The queues at the cash registers had seemed endless, and the whole excursion had taken much longer than Mrs Callahan had expected. The sun was just going down, and a brisk winter wind was blowing. The sky had completely clouded over, and it felt as though it might begin snowing at any moment.

"I hope poor Santa Paws isn't too cold," she said, as they crossed the car park. "If I'd known we would be stuck in there for such a long time, I really wouldn't have let him come."

Gregory looked worried. "It *is* a lot colder than it was before. Do you think he's OK?"

"I'm sure he's fine," Mrs Callahan said

quickly. "His fur is nice and thick this time of year."

As they approached their car, they could see a small crowd gathered around it.

Patricia shook her head in disgust. "Boy, sometimes he must get really tired of all this attention."

"He's a dog," Gregory pointed out. "Dogs love attention."

Just then, an Oceanport police car pulled up near the crowd, and two officers got out. At a distance, it appeared to be Officers Bronkowski and Lee. Because of Uncle Steve, the Callahans knew just about everyone in the department pretty well. Officer Lee was speaking into his radio, while Officer Bronkowski was walking over to the car. She had her torch out and seemed to be peering inside the back windows.

"Well, good," Patricia said. She was always pleased to see police officers on the scene. On *any* scene. It made life much more orderly. "We definitely need some crowd control here."

Then they heard a siren and saw a red flashing light as another squad car came roaring into the car park.

"Hey," Gregory said nervously. "They're acting like something's *wrong*."

Now, from a distance, they could hear another siren approaching.

"Hey," Gregory said again, as he started to get scared. The police cars wouldn't be using their sirens if they were just on a routine patrol of the mall.

Mrs Callahan abruptly put her shopping bags down. "Would you two mind watching these for a minute? I'll be right back."

Patricia and Gregory looked at each other with wide eyes. Yeah, they minded! Something bad had obviously happened, and they didn't want to wait all the way over here before they found out what it was.

"Mum," Patricia started, uneasily.

"Just wait here!" Mrs Callahan said, her voice sounding almost fierce.

Their mother rarely got angry at them, and so Patricia and Gregory didn't argue. They just stood quietly by the shopping bags while Mrs Callahan strode swiftly over to Officer Lee. In fact, she was walking so fast that she was practically running! She started talking to him, and then looked stunned by whatever he had told her. She pushed her way through the crowd, and joined Officer Bronkowski by the car.

"It's Santa Paws," Patricia said, practically whispering. "Something must have happened to Santa Paws."

"Do you think he *bit* someone?" Gregory asked, horrified. That was the worst thing he could imagine, because he knew his dog would never hurt anyone. Even if they were teasing him. But, why else would the police have come?

Patricia shook her head, feeling herself start to tremble. She realized now that her mother wasn't angry – she was *scared*. That must be why she had spoken to them so sharply.

Gregory let his parcels fall on the cement with a crash, even though a couple of them were fragile. "If it's about Santa Paws, I'm not waiting over here. *No way*."

Patricia grabbed his arm to pull him back. "Wait, Greg. Mum said—"

He shook her hand off roughly. "Since when do *you* do everything you're told? Leave me alone! I'm going over there."

The third squad car had arrived, and Uncle Steve and his lieutenant climbed out. Both men looked very solemn.

Patricia knew that when law enforcement *supervisors* showed up, that meant that things were serious. "OK," she said, making up her mind. "Come on." She bent to gather up a few of her mother's bags, adding them to her own load. "Grab as many of the parcels as you can."

Mutely, Gregory nodded, and they both hurried over to join the crowd of bystanders and police officers.

"What's happened, Uncle Steve?" Gregory asked, able to feel his heart pounding inside his chest.

Uncle Steve turned away from the car, carefully using his stick for balance. "We, uh—" He stopped. "We're trying to work that out, Greg. Don't worry."

Gregory and Patricia stared at him. Had he lost his mind? How could they possibly *not* worry?

"I'll tell you what's happened!" a boy in the crowd volunteered. "Someone's stolen Santa Paws!"

"Yeah, we saw it!" his friend said eagerly. "Two creepy men in a van! That's why we called the police!"

Unable to believe it, Gregory ran forward to see for himself.

"Don't!" Patricia ordered, as he reached out to open the back door. "There might be fingerprints!"

Gregory hesitated, his hand halfway to the door handle.

"She's right," Officer Bronkowski said. "Please don't touch anything, OK, Gregory? We're waiting for the crime scene unit to get here."

Gregory looked at the shattered window, and gulped back tears. How could a "crime scene" involve *his* dog? "I-is there any blood? Did they hurt him?"

Mrs Callahan put her arm around him. "No,

they wouldn't hurt him," she promised. "It's probably just someone playing a joke on us. Don't be scared."

"It was no joke!" the boy in the crowd said, seeming to enjoy his status as an eyewitness. "He was unconscious! We *saw* it!"

Gregory started crying then, covering his eyes with his hand. People had stolen and injured his dog! How could he ever have imagined that Santa Paws might have bitten someone? This was *so much worse*.

Furious that the boy had upset her brother so much, Patricia whirled to face him. She recognized him, and she was pretty sure he went to the high school. "Why didn't you stop them?" she demanded. "If you saw them, why didn't you do anything?"

"We called the police," the boy said defensively.

"They were *big*," his friend added, equally defensive.

Patricia glared at them. "*I* would have tried to stop them."

Uncle Steve's boss, Lieutenant Trent, was saying something in a low voice, and Uncle Steve nodded. He called over two other officers.

"Move the crowd out of here, all right, guys?" he said. "I want a thirty-metre perimeter, minimum."

"Sure thing, Sarge," one of the officers said,

while his partner nodded. Efficiently, they guided the curious onlookers away. In the meantime, Officer Lee was setting up some yellow crime scene tape to keep the area as clear as possible.

As other shoppers left the mall and saw all of the commotion, they came over to see what was going on. So even though the crowd was now further away, it was bigger than ever.

Gregory, Patricia, and their mother stood about three metres from the car and unhappily watched all of the activity. Gregory wasn't making a sound, but tears were still streaming down his cheeks. Mrs Callahan kept blinking, and had a handful of tissues clutched in one hand. Patricia's expression was blank, and the only sign that she was upset was how tightly her arms were folded across her chest.

"Did they set up roadblocks?" she asked Uncle Steve. "Barricade the motorways?"

He sighed. "It wouldn't help much, Patricia – we have absolutely no idea which way they might have gone, and too much time had passed before we got the word."

Patricia nodded, her face even more expressionless now.

"We put out a BOLO, though, to the entire state, and we're going to extend it throughout New England," he said. "BOLO" was police slang for "Be on the Lookout". "Every cop in the state is going to be watching for them."

The two boys who had witnessed the crime had been interviewed several times now, but they hadn't been able to provide any new details. The thieves had been heavy men in their thirties, and both had unkempt, dirty-blond hair. The witnesses were sure that the thieves had been driving a van, but one boy thought it was grey, and the other one was sure it had been brown. They both agreed that there hadn't been any markings on the side, and – to Patricia's disgust – neither had noticed the licence plate.

Mrs Callahan had borrowed Lieutenant Trent's mobile phone, and called Mr Callahan to tell him the terrible news. About fifteen minutes later, he arrived in the family's other car, which was an ancient Buick.

By now, the crime scene unit – consisting of a specially-trained officer and two lab technicians – was searching for evidence. Two spotlights had been set up so that they could see in the darkness. The lights in the car park weren't bright enough. They had found several clues, including a still-damp crumpled bandanna on the ground. Apparently, it had been soaked with chloroform, a drug which would have made Santa Paws pass out. One of the technicians cautiously picked the cloth up with a pair of sterile tweezers and dropped it into an evidence bag. The other technician was using special powders and sprays to try and find fingerprints on the car. Later on, the Callahans would all have to give fingerprint samples to be used for comparison. In fact, anyone who might have touched the car – from family friends to the petrol station attendant – would probably have to be fingerprinted, too.

"What are they doing?" Gregory asked shakily, as he saw a technician running some kind of ultraviolet light over the inside of the car.

Uncle Steve didn't answer until the technician straightened up and gave the "All Clear" sign. "That's a way for us to see if there's any blood or other fluids," he explained. "Now we can be pretty sure he isn't hurt, because they didn't find anything."

Gregory nodded, and rubbed a fresh tissue his mother had given him across his eyes. At least he knew his dog wasn't bleeding, but they *had* drugged him. What if they had given him an overdose? Or what if he was allergic to the drug, and it made him sick? Or maybe they had hit him, or – Gregory shook his head, hard. He didn't want to think about anything like that. He didn't want to think about anything at all. He just wanted his dog back, safe and sound.

Patricia didn't start crying until she saw a technician sealing Santa Paws' collar into a plastic bag. But once she started, she couldn't stop. She got into her father's Buick and buried her face in her arms, crying and crying.

"Look, there's nothing more you can do here," Uncle Steve said to Mr and Mrs Callahan. "Why don't you take them home, and I'll call you the second we hear anything. We're also going to send Officer Bronkowski along, to set up a recorder on your telephone. The Lieutenant wants all of your calls monitored."

Mrs Callahan looked shocked. "You mean, you think they might demand a ransom?"

"I *hope* so," Uncle Steve said frankly. "It'll make them that much easier to catch."

Gregory and Patricia didn't want to leave, but they were so upset that they didn't really want to stay, either. They put on their seatbelts and sat silently in the back seat, while their parents loaded all of the shopping bags into the boot. None of them really cared about Christmas right now, but there was no point in leaving all of their parcels behind, either. Once the investigation had been completed, one of the police officers would bring the car to a garage so that the shattered back window could be replaced.

The family rode in complete silence. Losing

Santa Paws was so awful that there really wasn't anything to say. Gregory and Patricia just kept crying quietly, and their parents were blinking and swallowing a lot. Mr Callahan even had to pull over once, to clean his glasses because they had misted up.

Gregory couldn't help hoping that all of this had been a mistake, and Santa Paws would be waiting at the front door when they got home. He didn't believe that it would really happen, but he wished with all of his heart that it would.

But, when Mr Callahan pulled into the drive, the front garden was empty, and no one was waiting at the door. The first thing Mrs Callahan did was check the answerphone, but no one had called them. They weren't even any hang-ups. If there was going to be a ransom demand, it hadn't come yet.

Gregory and Patricia went straight upstairs to their rooms. They didn't want supper and they didn't want to talk.

The only thing they wanted was their dog.

In the meantime, the beastly brothers, Chuck and Eddie Hawthorne, were speeding along Interstate Route 95 in their van. Santa Paws was still unconscious on the floor in the back.

"We're going to be rich!" Eddie gloated. "Man, I can't believe how easy this was!"

"Watch your driving, you dope," Chuck warned him. "You wanna get pulled over for speeding, with the merchandise in the back?"

"Yeah, yeah, yeah," Eddie mumbled, but he slowed down to about ninety kilometres an hour.

"That's better," Chuck said, and greedily crammed some crisps into his mouth. They had only driven about eighty kilometres, and he was already on his second bag.

Eddie, on the other hand, had a sweet tooth. So he had been chomping on Polos and chocolate, and slurping Cokes the whole way.

"How long will that dumb animal be out?" he asked, with his mouth full of M&Ms.

Chuck shrugged. "I dunno, I never done that before. Couple of hours, maybe. He wakes up and gives us any grief, we'll just dose him again."

Eddie burped, and reached for a Mars bar next. "He'd better be able to last till we get to Jersey. I'm not cleaning up after him – or taking him on no walks, neither."

"Hey, for fifty thousand bucks, we can afford some paper towels," Chuck said, "know what I mean?"

Both men laughed raucously at that. They gave each other high-fives, and then Eddie stamped harder on the accelerator. They were getting close to the Rhode Island border, and the sooner they got out of Massachusetts, the better. With each passing kilometre, Oceanport slipped further and further behind them.

If the Hawthornes had their way, Santa Paws would never see his home – or his family – ever again!

Chapter 6

As the evening wore on, Mr and Mrs Callahan kept waiting by the telephone, but it never rang. Officer Bronkowski had connected a special recorder to their answerphone, and stayed long enough to make sure they knew how to run it properly. That way, if the dognappers called, the Callahans would be able to keep a copy of the conversation. Officer Bronkowski had also set up a tracer line, which was connected to the switchboard over at the police station. Someone would be monitoring that line around the clock, ready to trace the location of any calls that came in. If the criminals tried to make contact, the Oceanport police were ready and waiting to respond!

As soon as Uncle Steve's shift ended, he came over to keep Mr and Mrs Callahan company. His wife, Emily, and little daughter, Miranda, would have joined him, but Miranda was only two and she was already in bed for the night.

There didn't seem to be much to say, so the Callahans and Uncle Steve just sat at the kitchen table and quietly drank cup after cup of coffee. The ticking of the clock on the wall seemed very loud.

In the meantime, Gregory and Patricia were still upstairs in their rooms. They had both changed into their pyjamas and climbed into bed. Gregory had turned his light out, and was holding their cat, Evelyn, while he cried. Every time he tried to stop, he would think about his poor dog, and start up all over again. Evelyn purred, trying to comfort him. She wasn't sure where Santa Paws was, but she knew there must be a bad reason why he hadn't come home from the shopping trip. She liked to pretend that she hated dogs, but actually, she loved her friend Santa Paws very much. She hoped that he would be home soon, and that everyone would stop crying.

Over in her bedroom, Patricia had her stereo headphones on, but she wasn't actually listening to anything. She just wanted to be left alone. She tried reading for a while, but she couldn't concentrate. So she gave up and stared at her ceiling instead. She had cried for a while, but now she was almost too sad to do it any more. All she knew was that she had never felt worse in her life.

Earlier, their parents had come upstairs with supper trays for them, but they just weren't hungry. Gregory drank his milk, and Patricia ate a couple of bites of butterscotch pudding, but that was all.

At about nine o'clock, the telephone finally rang once, but it was only Aunt Emily, wanting to know if they had heard anything yet. After that, a series of calls came in from reporters wanting statements, but whoever answered would just respond with a polite "No comment" each time.

Upstairs, alone in their rooms, Gregory and Patricia both knew that it was going to be a very long – and lonely – night.

The robbers continued speeding towards New Jersey in their van. Santa Paws was still unconscious, although the chloroform was starting to wear off a little. Eddie just cruised along the motorway in Connecticut, switching lanes constantly. He also liked to keep his headlights at the brightest setting, to annoy the other drivers.

"Hey, man, I'm getting hungry," he complained, after a while.

"Yeah, right," Chuck said scornfully. "Give me

a break – you've been pigging out on sweets for hours."

"So what?" Eddie pointed at a sign for a rest area. "Let's stop there. We need petrol, anyway, and we can get some food."

Chuck didn't want to take any chances, but his stomach was growling, too. He had finished his last bag of crisps back around New London. "Yeah, OK," he said reluctantly. "But anyone sees that dog, and I'll pound you!"

"You pound me, and I'll pound you right back!" Eddie warned him.

"Just shut up, and make sure you don't miss the exit," Chuck said, not very impressed by the threat. Eddie was mean, but when it came to fighting, he was *slow*.

They were about to go past it, so Eddie cut across two lanes of traffic. Horns blared all around them, and he howled with laughter.

"Gotcha, you chumps!" he yelled at no one in particular. Then he swerved into the rest area car park, knocking over a dustbin on the way. This made him laugh even harder.

"Park away from everyone else," Chuck instructed him.

"Like I don't know that?" Eddie asked. "What, do I look stupid?"

Chuck studied him for a minute, then nodded.

"Yeah. As a matter of fact, you do. *Unusually* stupid."

"Takes one to know one!" Eddie said, and cracked up again.

Before they got out, Chuck took the precaution of tossing an oil-stained piece of canvas over the unconscious dog. That way, no one would be able to see anything suspicious, if they happened to look inside the windows.

Santa Paws was dimly aware that the van had stopped, but he felt too sick to open his eyes. His stomach seemed to be spinning in circles, and it was hard to breathe. He tried to sit up, but he was so weak that he immediately lost consciousness again. The drug was still too strong for him to overcome.

The Hawthornes returned with several lottery tickets and enough food for at least half a dozen people. Big Macs, McNuggets, milkshakes, giant-sized orders of chips – if it was on the menu, they had ordered it. Except, of course, for the stupid salads. The Hawthornes *hated* salad. The only vegetable they liked to eat was onions, and they didn't even like those unless they were raw.

The brothers ate their food, and burped, and ate some more.

Under the oily tarpaulin, Santa Paws vaguely sensed the rich scent of meat. He opened his eyes briefly, then let them flutter shut again. For the first time in his life, the smell of food was actually nauseating. He was still too dazed to bother wondering where he was, or what was happening. All he knew was that he felt very ill, and that he kept passing out.

And with that, he fainted again.

Back in Oceanport, Mr and Mrs Callahan were exhausted from the stress of waiting for the ransom phone call that never came. Uncle Steve was going to stay the night, so he and Mr Callahan set up the sofa bed. Uncle Steve insisted he was only staying because they were family, but the Callahans knew he also wanted to make sure they had some police protection on the premises.

Once the sofa bed had been prepared, Mrs Callahan turned on the television in the living room. The news was just starting, and their beloved dog's disappearance was the lead story. Her eyes filled with tears, and she quickly flicked it off.

"I know you don't want to see that," Uncle Steve said, "but the more publicity this gets, the better. People will be keeping an eye out for him."

Mrs Callahan nodded, although she didn't believe that publicity would help. In fact, if Santa Paws had never got any publicity in the first place, he wouldn't have become so famous that someone would want to steal him. She would never share her fears with her children, but she was terribly afraid that they were never going to see Santa Paws again.

Gregory had long since fallen into a restless sleep, but just then Patricia came slowly downstairs. Her hair needed brushing, and her eyes were red from crying.

"I heard the phone ringing before," she said, without much energy. She knew that if there had been any good news, her parents would have raced upstairs to share it. "Has anyone seen him, or – or anything?"

Her father shook his head. "I'm afraid not, Patty. I'm sorry."

That was the answer she had expected, but it was still devastating to hear. "OK," she said dully, and turned to go back upstairs.

"Would you like something to eat?" her mother asked. "It might make you feel better."

"No, thank you," Patricia said, and trudged towards her bedroom.

Her mother followed her, so she could tuck her in for the night. But first, she gave her a big, warm hug.

"Lots of people are looking for him, Patricia," she said. "I'm sure we'll have good news tomorrow."

Since her mother was just trying to make her feel better, Patricia forced herself to smile.

"Try to get some sleep," Mrs Callahan said kindly. "We'll talk about everything in the morning."

Patricia nodded, and closed her eyes without another word.

After Mrs Callahan turned out the light, she went across the landing to check on Gregory. When she walked over to his bed, he woke up.

"Did they find him?" he asked eagerly. "Is he OK?"

"I'm sorry, Greg, but not yet," his mother said. "I didn't mean to wake you up."

Gregory sagged back down against his pillows. He had been having a terrible nightmare that Santa Paws was lost in the middle of a big city, and that no matter where Gregory searched, he couldn't find him.

"He's never coming back, is he, Mum?" Gregory said, fighting back another bout of tears.

Mrs Callahan sighed, and reached over to brush his hair back away from his forehead. "I don't know, Gregory," she answered honestly. "We just have to hope, and pray, that everything is going to be all right."

Gregory hoped that with all of his heart – but he didn't believe it for a minute.

* * *

The next time Santa Paws woke up, he was relieved to find that he was much less dizzy and lethargic. But it was still hard to breathe, and he was very confused. He seemed to be in some kind of vehicle which kept starting and stopping, and he could hear two harsh male voices arguing. And the constant back and forth motion was upsetting his stomach again.

He couldn't seem to see, or move, or – what was happening? Where was he? He tried to bark, but found that his mouth would barely open. Something uncomfortable was tightly fastened around his muzzle. Was it a new collar? But why would it be around his mouth? He brought a paw up to try and dislodge the strange object, but he had no luck. He was about to panic and whimper, when the strong human stench coming from the front seat made something in his memory flicker.

Now he remembered! It was the bad people! Had they taken him away in the Callahans' car? He must be in a car, because he could feel it moving, even though their progress seemed to be very jerky. One minute, the car would be rolling forward, and the next, they would slam to a stop.

Santa Paws sniffed the air some more, trying to make sense of his surroundings. This wasn't his family's car, because everything smelled unfamiliar. Motor oil, car exhaust, and what seemed to be months' worth of fast food rubbish. He must be in a car that belonged to the bad people, and they were taking him somewhere. Wondering if they might be driving him to the Callahans' house, he felt a flash of hope. But why was it taking so long? His limbs felt so stiff that he must have been lying on this cold metal flooring for *hours*.

Even though it was dark, he could tell that a coarse cloth which reeked of motor oil and axle grease was covering him. When the vehicle came to an especially short stop, the cloth slid off to one side and his head was exposed. The air inside the van wasn't very fresh, but it was much easier to breathe without being smothered by that suffocating canvas.

Where were Gregory and Patricia? Did they know where he was? Would they be coming to get him soon? What if the bad people had hurt them! He had to find them, right away! Keeping his family safe was the most important duty in the world!

He was going to jump up, but decided to stay where he was. Maybe he should try to work out what the bad people were doing, first. Also, what if they tried to make him smell that nasty medicine stuff again? He still felt very sick, and didn't want them to do anything to make him faint again. Fainting was too scary. Besides, the longer he stayed here quietly, the more strength he could feel slowly flowing back into his muscles.

Even so, it would be nice to jump up and bite both of the bad people, as hard as he could!

"You are so stupid," Chuck was complaining.

The van moved forward, then stopped abruptly, yet again.

"I am not," Eddie said, with a distinct whine in his voice. "Like it's my fault there's traffic? You think I'm, like, the Road God?"

Chuck shook his head with disgust as he stared at what looked like several kilometres' worth of an endless traffic jam ahead of them. At the moment, the motorway resembled a car park more than anything else. "More like the Road *Hog*," Chuck said. "I *told* you to take the Merritt Parkway. But, did you listen to me? No. Do you *ever* listen to me? No. And now, look at this mess! We're going to be here for hours, and it's all your fault!"

"Yeah, well, the Merritt Parkway's too twisty," Eddie said, in his own defence. "And there's all those dumb trees. It doesn't have no McDonald's or nothing, neither."

"It *also* doesn't have any traffic," Chuck reminded him.

"I don't like parkways," Eddie said stubbornly.

"And that one keeps changing names all the time. First, it's like, the Hutchinson, and then the Sawmill, and – it's just too hard. I figured, we stay on 95, and boom! Right over the George Washington Bridge, and then just another hour until we get our fifty thousand bucks. Then, hello, Atlantic City!"

"Look around, man," Chuck said, gesturing at the cars surrounding them. The other drivers were also impatient, and many of them were leaning on their horns. "This is the Cross-*Bronx* Expressway, you bozo. You know what that means? We're *in* the Bronx! You know how dangerous that is?" Since he was from a small town, *anything* about a big city was frightening to him, even though the Bronx was really a very nice place.

"I'm not scared of nothing!" Eddie bragged. "Anyways, doncha read the paper? New York's got no crime any more." Then he looked thoughtful. "Maybe we should move here. There must be good pickings, these days."

"Not me. City criminals got no class. Not like us." Then Chuck scowled and put his seatbelt on as his brother jammed on the brakes still one more time. "Watch where you're going, moron!"

"I am watching," Eddie insisted. "These dumb New Yorkers just don't know how to drive."

"Look who's talking," Chuck said.

Eddie slammed the van into "Park" so unexpectedly that they were almost rear-ended by the car behind them. "OK, fine. You want to drive?"

"No, I don't want to drive, you big baby," Chuck said, mimicking his whine perfectly. "Just get moving."

"You're so smart, *you* drive," Eddie said, and unlocked his door. "I'm sick of your griping."

Santa Paws sat up partway, very alert. He knew that the sound of a car door unlocking usually meant that someone was about to open it.

"You'd better not get out of the van," Chuck threatened him.

"I quit!" Eddie said. "Unless you feel like walking the rest of the way, *you* can drive."

"Fine." Chuck unbuckled his seatbelt. "You want to switch, we'll switch. It'll be a lot better than listening to your moaning."

Santa Paws tensed all of his muscles, preparing himself for action. If the bad people were really going to open the doors, he might be able to run away. Then he could find his family and go home where he belonged. Where he was happy, and safe.

Eddie got sulkily out of the van, leaving his door ajar. Several nearby drivers beeped their horns, but he just made rude faces at them.

The door was open! This was his chance! Santa Paws silently rose to his feet, shaking the canvas off and getting ready to make his move. Then he dived for the exit with every bit of energy he had.

It was now or never!

Chapter 7

Chuck must have heard something, because he turned around just in time to see Santa Paws lunging towards the driver's seat. Forty kilograms' worth of determined, airborne Alsatian was an intimidating sight, and his first reaction was to cover his face with his arms and cower in his seat.

"Eddie!" he screeched. "Get back here! The mutt's trying to escape!"

Santa Paws vaulted right past the cringing man. Chuck recovered enough to make a grab for his back legs and missed. The dog plunged through the open van door and landed painfully on the motorway below. He was slightly stunned by the fall, and had trouble getting up for a few seconds. The deadly chloroform was still in his system, and it had slowed both his reactions and his ability to think quickly. Santa Paws dragged himself to his feet, shaking his head to try and clear it.

Chuck had leapt out of the van right after him, and now Eddie ran to block his way from the other direction. Santa Paws looked back and forth, trying not to panic. He was trapped between the two bad men, and cars were hemming him in on the other side. He growled uneasily, although the sound was muffled by the leather muzzle.

Nearby cars started beeping their horns, since this tense man-dog confrontation was going to slow down traffic even more. Many of them were, after all, highly-strung city people, and unnecessary delays made them irritable.

"Come on, nice doggie," Chuck said, with his cruel smile. "Come here, doggie! I have a bone to pick with – I mean, *give* you."

As both men charged towards him, Santa Paws leaped up on to the bonnet of the nearest car just in the nick of time. Chuck and Eddie promptly banged into each other, which made them twice as enraged at Santa Paws. The driver inside the car was startled to see a huge dog appear on her hood and she blared her horn, trying to scare this canine intruder away. Santa Paws had no idea how menacing the muzzle made him look. The piercing noise of the horn hurt the dog's ears, and he jumped off the bonnet and right into the middle of the slow-moving traffic.

Cars swerved right and left, trying to avoid hitting the dog – and each other. But there was really no place for the cars to go in the heavy traffic, so there were several collisions. The traffic jam had become complete pandemonium. Santa Paws was aware that Eddie and Chuck were trying to chase him, but he was more afraid of getting run over by one of the cars or vans. He had never seen so many automobiles in his entire life!

The combination of glaring headlights and a chorus of horns was very confusing. Santa Paws knew he had to get away, but he wasn't sure where to go. No matter where he looked, he could only see an endless parade of traffic. Where was the pavement? Where was the grass? Grass was always safe. He had to find some grass.

Finally, he turned left and started running. As he bounded up on to a concrete barrier, he realized that there were even more cars on the other side of the motorway. These cars were driving very fast, and coming from a whole different direction. Baffled and afraid, he turned to go the other way. He had lost track of Chuck and Eddie, although he could still hear them yelling.

"Get back here or you'll be sorry, you cur!" Chuck bellowed.

"Yeah!" Eddie agreed, although he wasn't sure what the word "cur" meant. "That goes double for me!"

Where should he go? What should he do? As Santa Paws stood uncertainly in the middle of the motorway, one van came so close to hitting him that he actually felt the tyre brush against his side. It was time to get away from here!

Santa Paws ran as fast as he could, dodging traffic, until he came to a crowded exit ramp. Again, horns were beeping all around him, and cars and trucks were trying to steer out of his way. A Toyota crashed into the back of a BMW, and their drivers leaped out to yell at each other. Santa Paws raced towards the bottom of the ramp, his heart thumping wildly. This was so scary! He came to an intersection that seemed to connect hundreds of streets together all at once. Some of the streets led right underneath the motorway, while others spread out in a confusing pinwheel in front of him.

What was this strange, alien, concrete place? Why weren't there any houses? Or trees? Or gardens? Where had the bad people taken him? He wanted to go home! *Now.*

The dog picked the street that seemed to have

the fewest cars, and dashed down it at top speed. Soon he came across a pavement, and gratefully galloped along it, instead. Pavements were so much nicer than being in the middle of the road. He ran and ran, not sure if Eddie and Chuck were still following him. He turned corners, crossed streets, dodged down alleyways, and raced below scary bridges and underpasses. Finally, he ran out of breath – and strength – and knew he had to stop and rest for a minute.

He saw a dark, secluded alcove next to a wheelie bin and decided to hide there. He ducked inside, and then collapsed in the shadows, out of sight.

The dog had no idea where he was, but for now at least he was free!

Once he caught his breath, Santa Paws slept for what felt like a very long time. During the night, the temperature dropped until it was only about twenty degrees, with a wind-chill that made it feel even more frigid. The dog began shivering so hard that it woke him up. Since he always took turns sleeping on Gregory's and Patricia's beds, he couldn't work out why it was so cold. Usually, the blankets were warm and – wait a minute, where was he? This wasn't the Callahans' house!

Santa Paws looked around, blinking. Then the

memory of his horrible experience with the bad people came flooding back. He sniffed the air nervously, to check and see if the men were anywhere nearby. No. His nose was overwhelmed by foreign smells, but the distinctive unwashed stench of the two bad men wasn't among them. Yay! He really had escaped!

Now his biggest problem was going to be trying to work out exactly where he was. Or even *roughly* where he was. Sometimes, the Callahans went on outings to the city, but this place seemed different. There were lots of buildings and concrete, though, so this place must be *like* that. But, how was he ever going to find his way home?

Feeling lonely, he wanted to let out a little woof, but then he realized that he had another big problem. His mouth was strapped shut! He dug at the muzzle with both paws, whining in frustration. Then he rubbed his head against the chilly cement wall of his alcove. He rubbed so hard that his ear and cheek felt raw, but the muzzle didn't budge. He slumped down, whimpering quietly. Why had those men been so *mean*? He was used to people who *liked* him.

The wind was swirling around, and he pressed deeper into his narrow alcove. The alcove was really just a doorway, but it felt less exposed than lying out on the pavement. In a strange, spooky place, he knew he needed as much protection as he could get.

There was a scuttling sound over by a wheelie bin, and Santa Paws saw some ugly little animals rummaging around. They had stiff dark fur, long yellow teeth, and pink naked tails. They looked sort of like cat-sized mice, but he was pretty sure he had never seen this kind of animal before. He didn't like them much, either. They seemed creepy.

The little animals scurried, and squeaked, and rustled through bits of rubbish in the street. One of them came near his alcove, and the dog growled at it. With the muzzle on, he wouldn't be able to bite them, but maybe the growl would be fierce enough to scare them away. The rodent flashed its sharp teeth in return, but then backed off.

Santa Paws wanted to move and sleep somewhere far away from those creatures, but he felt safer staying where he was for now. He would just have to stay awake to make sure none of them wandered over again.

Watching the animals fight over scraps of spoiled, discarded food from the wheelie bin, the dog suddenly realized how hungry he was. And thirsty! When was the last time he had had any water? The drug had left a nasty taste in his mouth, and his tongue felt very dry. When the sun came up, he would have to go out and do some scavenging of his own. It had been a long time since he had been forced to survive on the streets – but he still remembered how to do it. Once he got rid of the painful strap around his mouth, he would be fine.

The small animals finally stopped fighting and snapping, and went scuttling off to find other rubbish to eat. Santa Paws was relieved to see them go. Maybe now he could get some more rest. Tomorrow he was going to start searching for the Callahans, and he would need as much energy as possible for that.

It was so cold that he curled into a tight ball and huddled against the doorway. He should have taken the time to find a park, or some other place like that where he could make himself a warm nest out of leaves. When he had been a stray before, he had spent most of his time sleeping in the woods. For a while, he had camped in a small cave, and he had also lived in an abandoned shed. It was when he had started sleeping up by the middle school that he had met Gregory and Patricia.

Thinking about his family made him start whimpering again. Did they miss him as much as he missed them? Were they worried? Were they *safe*? Would he ever see them again?

Feeling too miserable to try to sleep any more, Santa Paws just huddled in his alcove to wait for morning.

When the sun finally came up, Santa Paws was so tired and cold that he wasn't sure he would be able to get up. His joints and muscles were practically frozen. When it came to being a stray, he was really out of practice! He staggered to his feet and stood there for a minute, until he felt steady enough to try walking. For the most part, the streets were quiet, although a few vans drove past him as he wandered from street to street.

As the sun rose higher, people began to leave their homes to go to church, or work, or maybe do some shopping. Since it was a Sunday morning, the mood in the neighbourhood was more leisurely than usual. The few people who noticed him seemed to think he was dangerous, because they quickly veered out of his way.

Santa Paws walked endlessly, with his head down and his tail dragging. No matter which way he went, he seemed to end up near yet another motorway. He didn't like motorways, so he would have to turn around and head off in a different direction. Once, when he was walking under a flyover, a great thundering roar filled his ears. He flattened on the pavement, terrified. A great big machine pounded above him for what seemed like hours. It was bigger than a truck, or even a bus – and horribly loud. He didn't like this place *at all*.

Once the machine had gone, Santa Paws got up carefully. Would it come back? He wasn't waiting around to find out! He chose a new street to follow, wanting to put the monster machine as far behind him as possible.

He found a puddle in a street pothole and tried to lap up some water, but the muzzle was so tight that he couldn't open his mouth enough to drink. That meant that he wouldn't be able to eat, either. He would starve!

There was a low chain-link fence nearby, and he tried to hook the muzzle over one of the protruding wires to yank it off. The only thing he managed to do was scratch his already-raw cheek. By now, the muzzle felt like a vice! He was too hungry and thirsty to think clearly, so he started wandering aimlessly again.

Then he came upon a huge park, with tall fences and decorative stone walls. There were all sorts of intriguing smells coming from inside, and for a minute, he forgot how miserable he was. He stopped and sniffed the air. Animals! Lots of different animals! Some of the scents were familiar – he recognized goats, and birds, and rabbits, and squirrels. But what were all of those other animals? Was this a special home, just for animals? If it was, maybe he could rest here for a while.

The special animal preserve was surrounded by large car parks. Happy families were leaving their cars and getting off big city buses to go and visit the animals. Santa Paws watched wistfully, because the families looked so jolly and excited. They reminded him of the Callahans. He could see Christmas lights, too, which made him feel even more sad. He wanted to go inside and explore, but he couldn't see any other dogs, so maybe he wasn't supposed to go in there. It had never made sense to him that dogs were allowed to go into some places, and had to wait outside others, but he had learned to live with it.

He lurked at the edge of one car park, trying to stay out of sight. Along with the exotic animal scents, he could also smell food! Hot dogs, and popcorn, and other good things! There were rubbish bins here and there, and he knew that if it weren't for the hateful muzzle, he could fill his stomach with discarded food.

Some of the other animals might have been able to smell him, too, because he could hear various howls and screeches and roars. Santa Paws was wildly curious, but also a little afraid.

Instinctively, he sensed that a few of those animals were downright *ferocious*. Maybe that was why they were all locked up in there?

The dog decided that this place made him nervous. He didn't want anyone to come along and put *him* in a cage. He also couldn't stand being able to smell so much delicious food that he couldn't eat. It was time to leave this mysterious park behind!

Santa Paws started running, and he didn't stop until he came to yet another wide motorway. There didn't seem to be very many cars, but the ones he did see were driving very fast. Was there a way to cross this road safely, or would he have to go around it? That could take *hours*. He waited uncertainly by the side of the road, trying to make up his mind.

As soon as there was a break in the traffic, he tore across the motorway to the grassy divider in the middle. Then he stretched out on his side to catch his breath. At home, whenever he walked anywhere near the street, Gregory always said, "No, no!" and shook his finger at him. So Santa Paws knew that cars could hurt him if he wasn't careful.

But right now, since he was in the middle of the motorway, what choice did he have? He either had to go back – or go forward. The cars on the far side of the grass were coming towards him from the other direction, which was confusing. Why couldn't they all just go the same way on both sides? Santa Paws watched them pass for a long time, doing his best to judge their speed. He was fast, but those cars were a whole lot faster!

He waited until the road seemed clear, and then started across. But then a small delivery truck appeared out of nowhere! It was heading straight for him!

Chapter 8

Santa Paws put on an extra burst of speed just as the driver of the truck slammed on his brakes. The truck squealed to a stop, leaving a terrible smell of burnt rubber in the air. Santa Paws could hear a man shouting at him, but he kept running. Boy, that had been a pretty close call!

He ran until he found a couple of trees to hide behind. His heart was pounding away, and he couldn't pant very well because of the muzzle. He *really* needed a drink of water. Worn-out from his already eventful day, he collapsed on to the ground to take a nap.

When he opened his eyes, he was less tired, but *more* hungry and thirsty. He rubbed the muzzle against one of the trees, but it stayed stubbornly attached to his face. By now he knew that he would never be able to take it off by himself. He needed to find a nice person who would help him. And if he was lucky, maybe the person would know Gregory and Patricia, and help him get home!

Back in Oceanport, the Callahans' house was much quieter than usual. Uncle Steve had got up early, so that he could go home and see his wife and daughter before his next shift. But before he left, he called the police station to see if any reports had come in. A few lost dogs had been located overnight, but none of them were Alsatian crosses. There was also no sign of a grey or brown van carrying two stocky men with straggly blond hair. An APB – which was an All Points Bulletin – had been sent to every law enforcement agency in New England by now, but so far, no one had called Oceanport with any information. Uncle Steve promised that he would be following up on every aspect of the investigation. He would call them right away if he got any news at all.

After Uncle Steve had left, the Callahans went to Sunday morning mass. Patricia and Gregory wanted to refuse, but their parents looked so tired and unhappy that they decided to go without voicing any objections. The church was decorated for Advent, and looked very pretty, but none of the Callahans were in a holiday mood. It would be awful to have their dog stolen at any time of the year, but the fact that it was almost Christmas made the situation seem even worse.

Immediately after the sermon, Father Reilly offered a special intention for Santa Paws. He asked the entire church to pray for the dog's safe return, and reminded them of the many good deeds he had performed for the townspeople. He also announced that there was a list in the vestibule for anyone who wanted to volunteer to help look for Santa Paws.

Gregory had a hard time not crying, when he listened to all of the nice things Father Reilly was saying about his missing dog. It was nice to know that people all over town were sorry about what had happened, but that didn't make him feel any less sad. Patricia got so upset during Father Reilly's speech that she actually had to get up and leave the church for a few minutes.

After mass, everyone came up to the Callahans to express their sympathies and ask if there was anything they could do. One well-meaning woman even asked if they would like a little cocker spaniel from a litter her dog had just had. When Patricia heard that, she politely excused herself and went to wait in the car. Mrs Callahan just thanked the woman for her kindness and tactfully changed the subject.

When they finally got home, Mr Callahan tried to cheer everyone up by making cornmeal pancakes and bacon. There weren't very many things he knew how to cook, but he was a champion at making breakfast. No one was hungry, but they all did their best to eat since he had gone to so much trouble.

Even Evelyn looked dejected. Instead of trying to snatch a piece of bacon when no one was looking, she just curled up sadly on the kitchen rug where Santa Paws usually slept. She missed him very, very much.

"Can we please go and look for him ourselves?" Gregory asked. "Instead of just waiting around?"

"Of course," Mrs Callahan said. "As soon as you've finished eating, we'll go out driving, just in case."

Patricia looked up from her hardly touched plate, her face brightening unexpectedly. "Hey, I know! We could offer a reward!"

Mrs Callahan nodded. "That's a good idea, Patricia. Why don't you and your brother make up some posters, and then we'll get enough copies made to hand them out, and hang them in shops."

Feeling a little better now that they had something tangible to do, Patricia and Gregory quickly finished their breakfasts. Then they hurried upstairs to get to work on their computers. Hand-lettered posters weren't good enough for Santa Paws; they wanted these flyers to look *professional*.

While Mr Callahan did the washing up, Mrs Callahan pulled out the Yellow Pages. She looked up the phone number of every single animal shelter in the Greater Boston area, and wrote them down on a pad. If necessary, she would call every animal shelter in the country! With each call, she reported that her dog was missing and gave whoever answered a detailed description of him. Almost everyone she called had heard of the famous Santa Paws, and they assured her they were already keeping watch for him. Many of them also gave her other numbers to call, belonging to animal rights organizations and any other people who might be able to help.

Upstairs, Gregory and Patricia used a scanner to copy several very flattering pictures of Santa Paws. They were careful not to look at the pictures too closely, so they wouldn't get too distraught to continue. Then, using a graphics program, they created three different posters. They tried to make the signs as eye-catching as possible by selecting lots of bright colours and dramatic fonts, as well as some clip-art with Christmas designs. At the bottom of each flyer, they typed in their phone number, as well as the number of the main switchboard at the Oceanport police department, so people would know who to contact.

Then they printed out copies of each poster and proofread them for mistakes.

"I think we should put a thick border around the word 'Reward'," Gregory said. "That'll get people's attention. Maybe around 'Missing', too."

Patricia nodded, and added that to each of the master copies. For good measure, she also created a border to emphasize the name "Santa Paws". "While I'm finishing, why don't you go online," she suggested. "I know there are dog rescue groups, and you can post messages there – and maybe some of the AOL bulletin boards and chat rooms and stuff. Plus, all your regular message boards and newsgroups, too."

Gregory nodded, and left the room to boot up his own computer. "I'm going to send out an e-mail to everyone in my address book, too, OK?" he called.

"Yeah, that's good!" Patricia called back. "Ask them to forward it, if they don't mind. I'll send one from my address book, too."

Neither of them had their own websites yet, but later today, they could maybe ask their friends who *did*, if they could post announcements on their sites. The more links they could set up, the faster they could get the word out. Their parents had never seemed too fond of the Internet, but as far as Gregory and Patricia were concerned, they just didn't appreciate all of the exciting possibilities. Sometimes their mother used it for research, or to correspond with other teachers, but that was about it. Their father had only tried going on the web once, had found it much too vast, and refused ever to attempt it again.

Maybe none of this would help them find their dog, but it certainly couldn't hurt!

Santa Paws was still resting under the two trees near the big motorway he had crossed. Once he felt strong enough, he got up and began to walk again. He wasn't sure where to go, but he had to try and find some help. So he decided he would just wander around until he found someone very kind. Many of these streets had long rows of terraced houses, with tiny fenced gardens. The rest of the streets were crowded with small shops and fast food restaurants and shabby old blocks of flats.

Smelling fresh, hot pizza, he stopped in front

of one shopfront. Santa Paws loved pizza, and it also reminded him of his family, as they enjoyed eating pizza, too. He waited in front of the door, hoping that someone would stop and help him with the muzzle. Maybe they would give him a bite of pizza as well!

He sat very politely, with his best posture. He waited for what seemed like hours, but no one even really paused. A few people spoke to him, but for some reason, he couldn't understand what they were saying. They were using words he had never heard before. Many of them sounded cross, while others just acted frightened. He knew he hadn't done anything wrong, so he wasn't sure why they didn't like him.

Finally, a plump bald man came out of the pizza place. He was wearing a tomato-stained apron and carrying a broom.

Santa Paws stood up, and wagged his tail. Finally! A nice person!

"Get out of here!" the man said, and shook the broom at him. "You're scaring my customers away!"

Santa Paws cocked his head. Why was the man so upset? And why was he swinging that broom? Then the bristles smacked him across the snout, and he leaped backwards, very startled. Had someone just *hit* him? Why? Was the world just suddenly full of mean people? What was going on?

"Get out of here, you mangy dog!" the man said, and aimed the broom at him again. "Before I have to call the cops!"

Santa Paws dodged the blow and retreated away from the shop. Then he started running, with his tail between his legs. The broom itself hadn't hurt that much, but the idea that someone would want to hit him hurt his feelings terribly. He had always been a good dog. He *knew* he was a good dog! So why did all of these people think he was bad? It was very confusing.

He slunk along the streets, doing his best to avoid attention. A group of boys hanging around on a corner laughed when they saw him.

"Yo, pit-bull!" one of them said.

The other boys laughed and started throwing bottles and drinks cans at him. Most of them missed, but one of the bottles shattered on the pavement near his face and that unnerved him. Clearly, the best thing to do would be just to avoid people completely. For some reason, literally overnight, he had become their enemy. Was it like that when he was a stray before? It must have been, but he couldn't quite remember. He had never really *wanted* to remember those long, lonely months.

He passed a couple of dogs who were being walked on leads, but their owners nervously pulled their pets away from the unfamiliar, scruffy Alsatian. In their experience, only vicious animals ever wore muzzles. An elderly woman with a tiny terrier paused as though she might want to help him, but by now, Santa Paws was too scared and he just ran away.

It was getting dark. He was alone, and miserable, and had no idea where he was. The wind was picking up again, and his paws ached from wandering so many miles on pavement and asphalt. He was also so weak from hunger and thirst that he knew he had to lie down for a while. But it was very hard, in the middle of the city, to find a secluded place.

Then he saw a huge pile of rags stacked on top of a metal grate. There was a dented supermarket trolley next to the pile, stuffed with grimy plastic bags and other worn objects. As he approached the rags, he felt a stream of hot air rising up through the grate. Heat! He could get warm! Yay!

He jumped happily on to the pile of rags. Then, to his horror, the rags *moved*! Then the rags let out a rumbling bellow!

The rags were alive!

Chapter 9

Santa Paws was so shocked that he actually fell over in surprise. Finally understanding that the pile of rags was really a person dressed in lots of bulky layers of clothing, he scrambled to his feet. But as he tried to race away, a grimy hand wearing a torn work glove hauled him back.

"Hey, now, what's all this?" a raspy voice grumbled from inside the rags. "Can't a man get himself some sleep?"

The voice was actually rather pleasant, sounding more indignant than enraged. So Santa Paws relaxed a little, and waited to see what would happen next.

"What's the world coming to? Tell me that, will you?" the man asked, looking him right in the eyes. "Don't you know better than to wake a fella up?"

This man seemed odd, but at least he was friendly. His face was unshaven and his hair was badly tangled, so it was hard to tell what he really looked like, or how old he was. Santa Paws tentatively wagged his tail a few times.

"What's this here contraption you got on?" the man asked. "You a biter?"

Santa Paws wagged his tail a little harder. The muzzle was bothering him so much that, without thinking, he pawed at it again.

"I hear you, pooch. Don't much like being confined myself," the man said. "You gonna tear my hand up if I take that thing off?"

Santa Paws tilted his head, not sure what the man wanted to know. He recognized the tone of question, but that was as far as he could get with this one.

"*Sit*," the man said.

Finally! A word he absolutely knew! Maybe not one of his favourites, but nice to hear under the circumstances. Santa Paws wagged his tail again, and sat down.

"Are you a good dog?" the man asked.

The dog's eyes lit up. Someone had said "good dog" to him!

"Well," the man drawled, "I don't think you're a biter. And – serves me right if I'm wrong." He reached out to unbuckle the muzzle. His hands were very large, and the knuckles were swollen from the cold. It took him a minute to work the buckle loose, and then he pulled the restraint off. He examined the leather briefly, shook his head, and tossed it aside.

Santa Paws barked with joy. He could move his mouth again! It felt great! His jaw felt stiff from having worn the muzzle for so long, so he barked some more to loosen it up. It was lots of fun to bark, after so many hours of forced silence. Then he leaned forward and nuzzled his face against the man's hand.

"You got good manners, pooch, don't you?" the man asked.

Hearing the word "good", Santa Paws whipped his tail back and forth. He always *tried* to be good, so it was nice that this man had noticed.

"So. You get yourself lost, or you just down on your luck?" the man wondered aloud.

The heat wafting up through the grate was so enticing that Santa Paws squeezed next to the man, still wagging his tail. He loved people, he really did.

"It's right easy to get down on your luck," the man told him, with a sigh. "You make some stupid mistakes, maybe lose a job, disappoint your family – and if you have some bad luck, you can end up out on the streets, like me."

The dog's ears shot up. Had the man said "family"? Did he know the Callahans? How lucky he was to have found this person.

"Can't say I didn't get myself into this jam, but now, it's like nobody even *sees* me," the man went on. "They just walk on by, pretend I'm not here. Makes you feel pretty bad, I'll tell you. Especially this time of year."

Santa Paws watched him intently, trying to work out what he was saying. All he knew for sure was that this man felt as lonely and sad as he did.

"You're a real good listener, pooch," the man said.

Santa Paws had never heard the word "pooch" before, but he liked it for some reason. It sounded affectionate.

"Watch it now, little friend," the man warned. "I been on my own so long, I might just up and talk your ear off."

The warm grate felt so comforting that Santa Paws snuggled closer to the man. What a lot of clothes he was wearing! For all the dog knew, underneath the garments, the man was actually very thin. His *face* seemed thin, behind all those greying whiskers.

The man put his hand out. "I'm Roy. How are you, pooch?"

Santa Paws lifted his paw, and Roy shook it, looking delighted.

"You know how long it's been since someone shook my hand, pooch?" he asked. "I tell you, friend, you almost make me feel human again." He dug through his layers of sweaters and shirts until he located the remains of a packet of crackers. "I don't got much, boy, but can I offer you some dinner?"

Hungry as he was, Santa Paws took the cracker gently from his hand. Gregory and Patricia had trained him to be very careful about not snapping by accident. He crunched it up, and thumped his tail gratefully.

"Well, all right then! Dinner is served!" Roy said cheerfully.

They finished all of the crackers in no time. First Roy would eat one, and then he would offer one to Santa Paws. They took turns until the crackers were gone.

"Sorry, pooch," Roy said, crumpling the empty plastic wrapper. "Wish I could do you better, but that's all I got today."

Santa Paws wagged his tail. He *liked* this sad, nice man. He wanted to go and find a puddle somewhere and drink, but he knew the man hoped that he would stay for a while. So he stretched out on the grate, using the man's knee for a pillow.

"Well, now, I like a pooch that doesn't eat and run," Roy said, pleased. "Glad to see you'll sit a spell."

It was dark now, and a light freezing rain was falling. Roy pulled some newspapers out of his trolley to cover them both up. The newspapers weren't a perfect shelter, but they helped protect them a little.

As the long cold night passed, mostly they both dozed. Sometimes, Roy would wake up and start telling him long stories about his life, and the adventures he'd had, and how he had ended up becoming homeless. How he wished he could start again, and do things differently this time. Whenever he spoke, the dog watched him intently. Then when Roy got tired of talking, he would just pat Santa Paws and tell him that he was a good dog. Hearing that made Santa Paws feel very happy. What a wonderful new friend Roy was.

It was – almost – like being back with his family again!

The Callahans had spent all of Sunday afternoon driving from town to town and putting up their signs. Mrs Callahan had stopped at a photocopy shop on Main Street, and had five hundred copies made of each flyer. So now they had a total of fifteen hundred to distribute. They hung the posters in shops, stuck them to telephone poles, and handed them out to anyone who seemed interested. No one they asked had seen Santa Paws, but each person promised faithfully to keep an eye out for him. Some of them even asked for extra flyers to give to their friends. Mr and Mrs Callahan were quick to provide them with as many copies as they wanted.

It was a gruelling way to spend the afternoon, but putting up the posters was more productive than sitting glumly in the house and waiting for the telephone to ring. Or *not* ring, as the case might be. Seeing Christmas trees, and menorahs, and houses decorated with wreaths and twinkling lights seemed very depressing, under the circumstances. It was a constant reminder that Christmas was less than a week away, and none of them wanted to think about that right now.

"Someone will see him, right?" Gregory said as he hung a poster in the window of a laundrette. "With all these posters up?"

Mr Callahan nodded, and rested his hand on his son's shoulder. "Someone's bound to, Greg. We just have to be patient."

Gregory didn't want to be patient – and neither did Patricia, but they managed not to say so. They knew their parents were only trying to make this terrible situation easier for them.

As it was a school night, Mrs Callahan wanted them to get home early enough to have dinner and get a good night's sleep. They still had some posters left over, but their father suggested that they take them to school the next day and hand them out there. Mrs Callahan was going to do the same at the high school.

When they got home, the red light on their answerphone was flashing wildly.

"It's good news!" Gregory said. "I know it is!"

Worn out from the hours of driving and hanging posters, Patricia was feeling much less optimistic about things. In fact, she was downright irritable. "It's probably just a lot of stupid reporters pestering us again."

"No, it's good," Gregory insisted. "It has to be."

Unfortunately, all of the messages turned out to be from people who had called to say how sorry they were that Santa Paws was missing. The messages were very considerate – but they weren't good news. The last one was from Uncle Steve, reporting that they were still waiting for results from the crime lab, but should have them by the next morning.

Mrs Callahan made tacos for supper, because

that was one of Gregory and Patricia's favourite meals. The tacos were delicious, but there was hardly any conversation at the table. After dinner, Gregory and Patricia helped with the washing up. Then they went upstairs to get ready for bed, significantly earlier than usual. They didn't even argue about who would go online first. Their parents had had an extra telephone line installed when it was clear that their children were going to tie up the main line for hours on end when they were on the web. In return, Gregory and Patricia had promised to take turns using their computers. They had also promised that they would never argue about it, either. Tonight was probably the first time they had ever succeeded in *keeping* that promise.

First Gregory downloaded his e-mail to read off-line. Then Patricia did the same. They had lots of replies to their various postings and messages, but just like the answering machine, they were of the "sorry to hear about Santa Paws, hope someone finds him soon" variety. So far, none of the efforts to find their dog seemed to be helping at all.

After he had answered his e-mail, Gregory came into Patricia's room and sprawled unhappily across the bottom of her bed.

"Do you think he's OK?" he asked.

Patricia hesitated, but then nodded. There was no point in making her little brother feel worse than he already did. "They only took him because they think he's worth a lot of money. So, there's no way they'd hurt him."

Gregory had his own doubts, but he nodded too.

Patricia got up from her desk chair to come over and sit next to him. "Look, Greg, the one thing we know for *sure* is that he's a survivor," she said. "I mean, we've seen what he can do, right? He's like – Superdog."

Gregory smiled weakly. "Lassie."

"Exactly," Patricia said, her smile just as feeble.

They sat there quietly. Evelyn came ambling in to keep them company and – without arguing – they took turns patting her.

"Do you think he misses us as much as we miss him?" Gregory asked.

She might not be sure of anything else, but Patricia *was* sure about that. "Definitely," she said.

The next morning, when Santa Paws and the man woke up, they both yawned and stretched. Roy stood up and stamped his feet to get the circulation moving. Then he checked his trolley to make sure no one had come along and stolen his stuff during the night. He had so few possessions that he treasured all of them.

Santa Paws gave himself a vigorous shake, and yawned a few more times. The rain had stopped just before dawn, and his fur was mostly dry now. The sun was shining, and even though he was terribly hungry and thirsty, he felt quite content. After such a good night's sleep, he knew he was ready to try and find his way back home to his family. Would Roy come with him, maybe? Santa Paws trotted down the street a few steps, then waited to see if Roy was going to follow him.

"Time to make my rounds, pooch," Roy explained. "If I find enough cans, I can make me a few dollars. And there's soup over at the church today. You want to come?"

Come. That was another one he knew. Santa Paws trotted back over to Roy, even though he was eager to start his journey. He pawed his friend's leg, then ran a short distance away. He stopped and barked a few times.

Roy let out a resigned sigh, and smiled at him. "Looks like you got places of your own to go, huh, pooch?" He crouched down and held his hand out. "Come here, and let me say goodbye, OK?"

Santa Paws returned and sat down in front of him.

"Well, there's a good boy," Roy said, and patted him. "I hate to see you go, but it sure was nice having you around last night."

Santa Paws thumped his tail on the pavement.

Roy looked at him for a long minute. "You want to know a secret, pooch? Over at the church one time, the Reverend told me he could get me into some kind of job-training. And I said, 'Rev, you won't catch me doing *that* until I see a sign.' You know? Something to show me my luck might change?"

Santa Paws tilted his head to the right, and then to the left. His friend was talking to him very seriously, and he wished he could follow the conversation better.

"Now, I don't believe in signs," Roy said. "Figured there was no such thing. And the Rev said, you just have to know where to look."

Santa Paws leaned forward and gave his hand a friendly lick.

"Now, see, there you go," Roy said, and smiled. "Could be the Rev was right, and it's a long time since I looked. Think I just might have myself a talk with him today, know what I'm saying?"

Santa Paws wagged his tail.

"OK, then." Roy patted him one last time before straightening up. "You take care of yourself, y'hear, pooch? Good luck to you!"

The word "good" again! Santa Paws barked.

Roy went over to retrieve his trolley, then turned to wave at the dog. "See you around, pal," he said fondly, and began pushing his trolley down the street. "Merry Christmas, little buddy!"

Santa Paws watched him go, wagging his tail non-stop. Then he stood up and sniffed the air in every direction. He sensed, somehow, that his family was north of here. Instead of being over-whelmed and afraid, from now on he was just going to follow his instincts. And his instincts were telling him to head north.

The rain from the night before had left lots of puddles, and Santa Paws drank until his throat was no longer dry. Then he began to trot up the street, heading directly north.

He was on his way to find the Callahans!

Chapter 10

Over the next few hours, the dog covered a lot of ground. He set a nice, steady pace, pausing only to drink from a puddle occasionally. By moving in an easy trot, he wouldn't get too tired. He did his best to head directly north, with maybe a slight tilt to the east. It just *felt* right.

Gradually, he left the city behind. It was a big relief to find himself in a more suburban setting. The streets were quieter, there were fewer cars, and he was able to cut through grassy gardens. Two days of constant contact with hard cement had really made his paws sore.

For a while now, he had been able to hear the noise of a crowded motorway somewhere off to his right. He wanted to avoid it, but soon found that he had no choice but to cross. That is, if he wanted to stay on course. He whined uneasily, striding back and forth on the hard shoulder. The traffic seemed very heavy and he was afraid to go anywhere near it.

Not sure what else to do, he continued along the side of the road for a while, even though it was taking him out of his way. The cars were driving so fast that he cringed almost every time one passed him. Then he came across a ramp, which led up to a flyover. A bridge! He could get across the motorway!

There were some cars on the entrance ramp, but he soon found an opportunity to rush across to the thick undergrowth on the other side. The flyover itself had a pavement, which made him very happy. From now on, if he needed to cross any more scary motorways, he would be sure to look for one of these special bridges! Soon the motorway was just a bad memory, and he was able to resume his determined trek through the suburbs.

The houses he was trotting by now were big and comfortable, sitting on large plots of land. The gardens at home in Oceanport weren't usually quite this big, and there was no comforting smell of the sea. Even so, he felt confident that he was on the right path.

Every so often he paused to drink from a small

puddle. It was getting colder, and a thin film of ice was beginning to form across most of them. But the ice was easy enough to break with his front paws and then he could drink his fill. In one garden, he even found a dustbin filled with delicious leftovers! He knew it was bad to knock over rubbish, but he was too hungry to worry about it. He gobbled down some cold potatoes and limp salad, along with a few pieces of stale bread. There were some pork chop bones, too, but most of the meat was gone.

The dog was just settling down for a nice chew when a man came out of a nearby house and looked angry when he saw the torn-up rubbish.

"Bad dog!" the man said. "Go home!"

Since he knew he *was* being bad, Santa Paws slunk away immediately. He didn't even remember to bring any of the bones with him. Further down the street, a large golden retriever boldly barked at him from behind a white picket fence. Santa Paws wagged his tail to show that he wasn't a threat and continued on his way. The retriever only barked a couple more times before losing interest and returning to her front porch for a nap.

Next, Santa Paws came to a golf course. Despite the chill in the December air and the grey overcast sky, there were a few die-hard sportsmen out there playing. Santa Paws stopped when he saw a small white object hurtling through the air towards him. What was it? Oh, a ball! What fun!

The ball gracefully arced down towards the ground, heading for a little hole with a flag sticking out of it. The ball landed directly inside the hole, with a small clatter against the sides. Santa Paws galloped joyfully over, knowing exactly what he was supposed to do with balls. People liked him to fetch them!

He nosed around inside the hole until he was able to grab the ball between his teeth. It was very small and hard – not nearly as nice as a tennis ball felt in his mouth. But he ran to return it to its owner right away.

Two men were hurrying across the brittle grass, hauling their golf bags on small wheeled carts. Instead of coats, they were wearing heavy sweaters, close-fitting leather gloves, and jaunty plaid caps.

"A hole in one!" the taller man was saying triumphantly. "I saw it go in! I'm sure of it!"

"Could be," his friend agreed. "We'll see when we get there."

The tall man was terribly excited. "I can't believe this! I've been playing since I was nine years old, and I've never hit one. Wait until my wife hears!"

Since the men were coming in his direction, Santa Paws decided that it must be their ball. He ran up to them and dropped it at their feet. Then he wagged his tail proudly, and waited for praise.

The tall man looked shocked; his friend laughed.

"I can't believe it," the tall man said softly.

His friend was still chuckling. "Well, Keith, I guess we'll never know."

Santa Paws was puzzled by their reactions. Weren't they happy? He had saved them the trouble of going all the way over to that hole to try and find such a tiny ball by themselves. Did they think he was bad? The very thought made his ears go down.

"I really want to yell at this dog," the tall man said finally, "but he thinks he did a clever thing, doesn't he?"

His friend nodded, laughing.

The tall man sighed, but then reached out to give Santa Paws a light pat. "OK, good dog. I'm sure you meant well."

Santa Paws wagged his tail, pleased that they thought he was good. What a relief! Then he barked once, and resumed his steady trot north. The two men watched him go.

"I think my wife might find this story a little bit too funny," the tall man said.

"I think so too," his friend agreed, and laughed some more.

A few minutes later, Santa Paws had crossed the outside edge of the golf course. Now he was back to travelling through peaceful neighbourhoods, as well as a few commercial streets. A couple of people noticed him, and shouted, "Hey, dog!" or "Come here, pup!" Santa Paws wagged his tail pleasantly at each of them, but kept going. Soon he saw a good-sized lake and stopped for a nice long drink. The water was very cold, but it tasted good.

It was beginning to get dark now, and the dog was getting tired. Soon, he would have to choose a good place to sleep for a while. But every minute he rested meant it would take that much longer to find his family!

After crossing a fairly busy road – his legs stiff with tension the whole time – he found himself on another golf course. Or *was* it? Could he have got lost, and gone in a circle? Santa Paws stood still to sniff the air, holding one paw up uncertainly. No, this was a different course, because there was nothing familiar about it. By now it was too dark to play, so he didn't pass any golfers as he loped over the grass. There were small clusters of trees, then wide sections of winter-dry grass with sandy areas and small ponds here and there. He paused, trying to decide if he wanted to sleep in some of that sand. It would be nice and soft. But, no, he wasn't quite ready to stop yet.

Once he had left that golf course, he came to another – and then another! What a strange town this was! There seemed to be more golf courses than houses! But maybe it would be fun to live around here, because there would be so many little white balls to chase.

Another motorway was looming up on his left side, and Santa Paws slowed to a walk. Could he face trying to cross another scary road right now? After such a long day? Maybe it *was* time to rest. His stomach was rumbling, but he couldn't smell any food nearby. He would just have to go to sleep hungry.

He went back to find one of those sandy pits and dug a hole big enough to fit his body. Then he turned around three times, the way he always did, and curled up. At first, the sand felt chilly and he thought about moving. But he was too tired, and his body heat was starting to warm the hole up, anyway. It was easier to stay where he was.

Curled up alone in the darkness, Santa Paws thought about Gregory and Patricia. Would he find them tomorrow, maybe? He felt as though

Oceanport was very far away, but he couldn't be sure. But he just missed them *so much*. And there was something particularly lonely about being here on this deserted golf course, with nothing but the faint sound of speeding cars to keep him company.

The dog whined a couple of times, then closed his eyes. He knew that he was facing yet another cold, lonely night. The only good thing was that the sooner he fell asleep, the sooner it would be morning again.

At home in Oceanport, Uncle Steve had come over that afternoon with good news. The crime lab had got a "hit" – or match – on a couple of the unidentified fingerprints the technicians had collected from the car. They belonged to a small-time thief named Chuck Hawthorne, who lived just north of Boston in the town of Revere. It turned out that he had a long history of committing crimes with the help of his little brother Eddie. They looked like even stronger suspects when a trace at the Massachusetts Department of Motor Vehicles showed that Eddie owned a six-year-old van!

The Revere Police were already on their way to the house where the brothers lived with their ill-tempered mother. They were planning to arrest the Hawthornes on suspicion of dognapping. If

121

they were successful, the hoodlums would then be transferred up to Oceanport for questioning.

"Can I interrogate them?" Patricia wanted to know. "I know just what to ask!"

Uncle Steve glanced at Mr and Mrs Callahan, and then smiled. "Well – it's an idea, Patricia, but I don't think we should go that way. We have to be very careful with our procedures to make sure everything will hold up in court later."

"I would only ask questions," Patricia assured him. "I wouldn't, you know, physically threaten them."

Gregory nodded. "Yeah, I bet!"

Patricia flushed, since – OK, she watched more than her share of television. Especially police dramas.

"I appreciate the offer, Patty," Uncle Steve said, his eyes amused. "But you're just going to have to trust us to handle it ourselves, OK? We do this for a living." His pager went off, and he looked down to check the number. "That's my lieutenant. I'd better check in."

Gregory and Patricia watched eagerly while he spoke on the phone. From his expression, it seemed as though he must be getting happy news. Uncle Steve hung up, looking elated.

"OK, we're in business," he said. "Some state troopers spotted their van in a car park near the

Massachusetts motorway, and arrested them when they came out." He pulled on his heavy police jacket and reached for his stick. "They're bringing them up now. I'd better get over to the station so I can meet them. I'll call as soon as I have more information."

Mr Callahan clasped his brother's shoulder. "Thanks, Steve. We really appreciate how hard you're working on this."

"Hey, I wouldn't even be standing here right now if Santa Paws hadn't saved *my* life once," Uncle Steve said. "I don't just love that dog, I *owe* him."

"Don't let them get some clever lawyer!" Patricia warned him.

Uncle Steve, who was halfway down the front steps, just laughed. Then, with a cheery wave, he left.

Gregory and Patricia exchanged huge grins. It was the first time they had felt happy since Saturday. They were trying not to get their hopes up too high, but it was almost impossible to avoid. Now that the police had apprehended the thieves, it meant that Santa Paws would be home soon. Maybe even tonight!

Santa Paws was sleeping restlessly in his sandy hole on the golf course. The combination of being hungry, cold, and sad made it very hard to relax. But he knew he needed to conserve his strength. Resting was the most practical way to do that.

Then, out of nowhere, there was a terrible sound of squealing car brakes, and he woke up with a start. What was *that*? He heard metal crunching, glass shattering, and tree limbs snapping. After a last dull crash, this was followed by complete silence.

Realizing that something bad had happened, the dog got up to investigate. The horrible sounds had come from the motorway, and so he made his way in that direction. Soon he came across the crumpled, steaming remains of a car. It had skidded off the road and down an embankment until it slammed into a tree.

The dog was very afraid of cars, but he knew he had to make sure everything was all right. He ventured closer, pausing to sniff the air every few steps. There was someone inside the car, but the person didn't seem to be moving. Santa Paws approached the driver's side and barked softly. The man inside was slumped against the steering wheel, unconscious. It wasn't good when people were very still like that! There was blood on his face, too. Blood was bad.

Very concerned now, the dog barked more loudly and pawed at the window. The man didn't respond in any way. Santa Paws tried a few more times, and then gave up. He knew that he had to go and find help.

Fast!

Chapter 11

The area seemed so isolated that Santa Paws wasn't sure where to go. He hated motorways, but that seemed like his best chance. He scrambled up the embankment, and began barking at each car that passed. It was fairly late, so there actually weren't very many. None of them slowed down, so they must not have seen or heard him.

For a second, the dog considered standing in the middle of the road to attract their attention. He took two steps forward before changing his mind. It would be too easy for one of those cars to hit him that way!

No, he needed to find a house where nice people lived. Then maybe he could get them to come and help the man in the car. There were street lights up ahead, and he raced towards them. Good! There were houses here! Most of them had their lights out, though. He knew that meant that people were sleeping, and he shouldn't wake them up.

One of the houses *did* have lights on, and he dashed up the front path. But then he heard what sounded like a ferocious Great Dane barking and growling inside. Not wanting any part of *that*, he wheeled around to go and find a different house. He took shortcuts through gardens, and heard other dogs bark at him. They were very *lucky* dogs, since they were safe at home with their owners. But, he didn't have time to think about that right now. Not with that man in trouble.

Around the next corner, he saw a house with plenty of lights on downstairs. He ran down the drive and began pawing at the side door, barking frantically the whole time. He kept barking at the top of his lungs until someone came to the door to see what was going on.

It was a woman in her late forties with dark brown hair, wearing a flannel nightgown and slippers. She peered outside, and then opened the door.

"What's wrong?" she asked.

Santa Paws wagged his tail, and barked.

"Whose dog are you, boy?" she asked curiously. "You don't look familiar."

Santa Paws barked, ran away a few steps, ran back, and barked some more.

Now a sleepy-looking man came to join the woman. "What's going on, Nancy?" he asked, putting on a pair of glasses so he could see better.

His wife shrugged. "I don't know. I can't remember seeing this dog around here before, can you?"

"No." The man yawned. "Look, I'm sure he'll calm down if we just leave him alone. If he keeps barking like this, he's going to wake the whole neighbourhood up."

Seeing the man lift his hand as though he were about to close the door, Santa Paws barked more urgently. Didn't they understand? A man needed help, and they had to come, right away!

"Maybe he's lost," the man guessed. "I'll call the police, and they can send an animal control officer over."

"You'll do no such thing, George!" his wife Nancy said firmly. "If he's lost, we'll take him in for the night, and decide what to do tomorrow."

George winced. "Oh, the cats are going to *love* that."

Nancy leaned down, snapping her fingers encouragingly. "Come here, boy. You can come in, it's OK."

Since she seemed to be receptive to him,

Santa Paws grabbed her dressing gown gently and tried to tug her outside. Then he let go of the cloth, and repeated his run up and down the drive, barking.

"He's crazy," George said.

Nancy put her coat on over her nightgown. "Well, he's obviously trying to tell us something. I'm going out there to see what he wants."

"Dressed like that?" George asked.

His wife nodded.

"*You're* crazy," George said.

Nancy was already halfway down the drive, following the frantic dog. George sighed and grabbed his own coat so he could go along.

Santa Paws led them back towards the motorway. He stopped every few metres, just to make sure that they were still close behind. George grumbled about having to climb around the woods in his slippers, but Nancy plunged right in. When she saw the car, she caught her breath.

"George, call 999! There's been an accident!" she said. "Hurry, and I'll see what I can do until you get back."

George turned and ran to their house, his slippers flapping against the street with each noisy step.

"Don't worry, boy," Nancy said to Santa Paws. "We're going to get some help for your owner."

She peered into the car at the unconscious man. The driver's side door was badly dented, but she was able to open the passenger's side. She climbed partway into the car to make sure the man was still alive. "Sir? Hello? Are you all right?"

The man didn't move, but the sound of his breathing was strong and regular. Nancy knew enough about first aid not to try to touch the man or move him. In a serious accident, it was always best to call an ambulance and wait for professional help. For now, she just took off her coat and used it to cover the man. It would help him stay warm until the paramedics arrived.

"Don't worry, mister," she said, even though she wasn't sure if the man could hear her. "The ambulance is on its way."

Outside the car, Santa Paws was too edgy to sit down, so he paced around. Was the man going to be OK now? Was this nice lady going to help him? Had he done the right thing?

George came lumbering back from their house, out of breath.

"They'll be here any minute," he panted.

"Good," Nancy said. "I think this poor man's in pretty bad shape."

George nodded, and then gave her his coat since she was shivering. "The guy's lucky to have such a clever dog. Do you think he got thrown from the car?"

Nancy started to nod, then frowned. "Actually, I don't know. The doors were all shut. The windows were closed, too."

"Well, he obviously got out *somehow*," George said.

Nancy nodded, and bundled her coat more closely around the injured man.

Santa Paws was the first one to hear the sirens, and his ears pricked forward. A minute or two later, George and Nancy heard them, too. George, who had brought a torch from the house, went up to the road to flag them down. It was actually the Hutchinson Parkway in Westchester County, which meant that Santa Paws had managed to travel pretty far that day. He was much closer to the Connecticut border than he had any way of knowing.

Then paramedics and police officers were climbing down the embankment. Santa Paws edged away a few metres. Seeing so many unfamiliar strangers all at once made him nervous. From their uniforms, he recognized that they must be people like Uncle Steve, but none of them looked or smelled familiar. So he decided to play it safe and keep his distance.

The paramedics performed a quick examination

of the injured driver. His vital signs were all strong, and they carefully fitted a supportive surgical collar around his neck to protect it. While they worked, the police officers interviewed George and Nancy. They were surprised to hear about the brave and loyal dog who had so cleverly saved his master's life, and they took detailed notes for their reports.

Just as the emergency medical technicians were strapping the driver to a backboard, he began to regain consciousness.

"Wh-where am I?" he asked. Then he groaned and tried to reach up and touch the bump on his forehead.

"Take it easy, sir," one of the paramedics said. "You've been in an accident, but you're going to be just fine." She did a few quick neurological tests and then nodded encouragingly at her partner. The man really *did* seem as though he would be OK.

"That's quite a dog you have there, sir," her partner said to the man. "He saved your life!"

The driver looked even more confused. "Dog? What dog?"

The paramedics looked worried, and repeated the series of neurological tests. Luckily, they got the same good results. Still, they couldn't help wondering if their patient might be suffering from some amnesia.

Now Nancy stepped forward. "Don't worry, sir, my husband and I will take your dog home for the night. We'll leave you our number, and you can pick him up as soon as you're feeling better."

"But I don't *have* a dog," the man said peevishly. "I don't even *like* dogs."

It was quiet, while everyone thought that over. Then one of the cops broke the silence.

"Well, maybe you should *start* liking them," he said, and everyone else nodded.

Nancy looked around to see where the dog was. If he didn't belong to the man, then maybe he really was lost. It was hard to believe that a stray would suddenly decide to rescue a complete stranger, but there was no other logical explanation. In any case, she wanted to make sure a great dog like that got home safely to his owners. And if he turned out to be an abandoned animal, then she and George would just keep him!

"Here, boy!" she called. "Where are you, boy?" She turned to her husband. "George, where did he go? We have to find him."

George shrugged. "I don't know. He was here a minute ago." He swung his torch back and forth, in case the dog was hiding nearby. "Come here, boy!"

The paramedics were carrying the driver up to the ambulance, so most of the police officers were now free to help search for the dog. They all fanned out into the trees, trying to catch a glimpse of the heroic stray. They searched, and called, and searched some more.

But the dog had gone.

Wide awake from his adventure, Santa Paws decided to continue his journey north. If he got tired, he would just stop and sleep somewhere. But he might as well take advantage of this burst of energy. He *did* wish he weren't quite so hungry.

In some ways, it seemed much safer to travel at night. There wasn't much traffic, and if there were bad people around, they would have a hard time seeing him. Of course he was used to sleeping at night. Then again, he was also used to sleeping most of the day! Adapting to all of this running around was a big change for him.

He soon discovered that there was *one* small problem about being out after dark – most of the local wildlife was awake, too! He came upon a raccoon unexpectedly, next to a narrow creek, and they were both so flustered that they ran in opposite directions.

When he caught a whiff of skunk, he knew he had to give *that* animal a wide berth. Once he had got sprayed in the garden at home, and Gregory and Patricia had given him about four baths in a row afterwards. Not only that, but they had used sticky tomato juice instead of water for two of them. Santa Paws hated baths, so he had vowed never to get near one of those black and white creatures again.

Later, he saw two deer in a small grove of trees, nibbling at some weeds. Then they bounded away on long skinny legs that were both elegant and also oddly awkward. The dog wasn't sure why he had made them so nervous, but he decided not to worry about it. Then, as he loped along through the darkness, he stepped on some broken glass by accident. It hurt a lot! Ow!

After putting weight on his right front paw, he realized that a sharp piece of glass was still stuck there. The dog stopped to see if he could pull it out. The glass was embedded deeply, and he had to gnaw at the piece for a couple of minutes before he could work it free. In the process, he cut his tongue a little bit, and whimpered. His paw was bleeding, and he licked the pads gently until the flow slowed down.

Then he stood up, cautious about putting his weight on that paw. It was painful, but not too bad. He didn't even really need to limp. So he started off again. From now on, though, he would try to be more careful about watching where he stepped. On a journey this long, he couldn't afford to injure himself. Things were difficult enough without adding *that* to his troubles!

Before long, the sky began to get brighter. The dog was getting tired and his trot had become more of a fast walk. His cut paw was aching, too. It was time to start searching for a nice, secluded spot to sleep. A spot *out* of the biting wind, if possible.

He noticed that there were folded newspapers in front of many of the houses he was passing. The newspapers had been dropped out near the street, which didn't seem right to him. At home, the Callahans' newspaper was placed neatly at the end of the drive in the morning. Santa Paws always liked to be the one to bring it inside the house. Whenever he was awake, Mr Callahan also let him go out to fetch the post from the postman, too. The dog felt good when he had special little tasks to do.

He was exhausted from his long night, but it still bothered him that these newspapers were in the wrong place. He should move them. So, at each house, he bent to pick up the newspaper on the pavement. Then he would run up to the front door, let it plop down nearby, and move on to the next house.

He was almost at the end of the road when he came to a small, well-kept white house with shiny black shutters. An elderly woman named Mrs Steinberg lived there. Mrs Steinberg was an early riser, and she enjoyed reading her morning newspaper with a cup of hot tea and some rye toast. Her paperboy, Todd, didn't have a very good throwing arm, so every day, her newspaper seemed to land in a different spot. Sometimes, she even had to dig it out of the bushes or from the flowerbeds. Luckily, Todd was extremely polite and likeable, so this bad habit didn't bother her all that much.

Santa Paws grabbed Mrs Steinberg's newspaper and ran up her cobblestoned front path. He was just about to drop it on the welcome mat when the door suddenly opened. He and Mrs Steinberg looked at each other in complete surprise. Then Santa Paws wagged his tail and deposited the newspaper directly into her hand.

"Well – thank you," she said, recovering from her amazement. She glanced around, but there was no sign of Todd – or anyone else, for that matter. "Good dog, I mean."

Santa Paws barked once, and then trotted towards the next house. He still had three more papers to redeliver.

Then it would be nap time!

Chapter 12

The night before, the Callahans had been very unhappy when they went to sleep. The news that the dognappers had been apprehended had seemed so promising, but it hadn't worked out that way. Over at the police station, the Hawthorne brothers were interrogated for several long, discouraging hours. They were kept in separate rooms, so the police could find out if their stories matched.

Chuck Hawthorne, the elder of the two, just sneered a lot and kept demanding fresh cups of coffee and high-fat snacks. The only answer he gave to any question the police asked was, "I don't know." Luckily, Eddie was not as tough as his brother was. At first, he denied everything, but then he gave a complete confession. He even identified the eccentric millionaire who had hired them to commit the crime in the first place. The man's name and address would be faxed down to the appropriate police department in New Jersey, so that he could also be arrested.

When Chuck found out that his brother had caved in, he reluctantly confessed, too. This would have been wonderful news, except that both thieves said that Santa Paws had escaped from them on the Cross-Bronx Expressway. They had got off at the next exit, and driven around for a while to try and find him. When they had no luck, they gave up and came back home to Massachusetts. They were very angry that they had lost out on their fifty thousand dollars. And their trip to Atlantic City!

So Santa Paws was no longer in any danger from the criminals, but he *was* lost in a huge, often apathetic city. And – he was more than three hundred kilometres away from home!

When Uncle Steve had called with this updated information, at first the Callahans were happy. Their dog had got away! Then, realizing what that meant, their happiness faded. In a city of more than eight million people, it would be close to impossible to find one lost Alsatian cross.

"Are you *sure* we can't go to New York to look

for him?" Gregory asked the next morning at breakfast.

The family had discussed this at length the night before, and Mr and Mrs Callahan decided that it just wasn't practical. New York was so big that they could search for *months* and never have any luck finding him.

"Your father's going to keep making phone-calls this morning," Mrs Callahan promised. "We'll get in touch with every animal shelter and police precinct in New York, to find out if anyone has seen him. And we'll just keep calling around, until we get some news."

Patricia and Gregory wanted to stay home from school to help call, but their parents didn't like that idea, either. They thought it would be better for them all to try and keep their lives as normal as possible. Patricia and Gregory weren't happy about this, but they just nodded glumly and pretended to eat their breakfasts.

Before it was time to leave for school, they went upstairs to check their e-mail yet again. Lots of people had been writing back to them, asking if they would send along a file attachment with a picture of Santa Paws. That way, their e-mail buddies – who lived all over the country – could print it out and make their own "Please Find Our Dog" signs. Patricia and Gregory were happy to do it, since they decided that there was no such thing as *too much* help in a situation like this.

"He doesn't know enough about cars," Gregory said unhappily. "How's he going to make it in a place like New York?"

Patricia had been thinking the exact same thing. "I don't know, Greg," she said honestly.

Gregory didn't want to start crying, because then he would have to go to school with his eyes all red. So, he rubbed his sweatshirt sleeve across his face to try and keep the tears back. "You think he'll try to come home?" he asked, his voice muffled by his arm. "Dogs do that sometimes."

Patricia decided not to point out that dogs did that in films. She wasn't sure if it happened in real life. She sighed. "I just don't know, Greg. I hope so."

She knew that it wasn't very likely, but it was also probably the only way they would ever see their beloved dog again.

So tired that he was practically stumbling, Santa Paws finally curled up behind a stranger's garage to sleep. It was fairly well-protected from the wind, and he was able to burrow into an old compost heap for warmth. He slept all morning and into the early afternoon, without moving or even dreaming. He was just too exhausted for that. Running so many kilometres during the past three days had really taken a toll on his body.

When he finally woke up, his stomach was so empty that it was actually painful. He *hated* being on his own like this, he really did. He felt so sorry for himself that he had to whimper quietly for a while. And his paw hurt, too.

With an effort, he dragged himself to his feet. Then he trudged out to the street and started on his way north again. Whenever he saw a dustbin, he paused to sniff hopefully, but they always seemed to be empty. He had vaguely heard the noise of a big, grinding truck while he was sleeping. It must have been a dustcart, picking up all of the nice, delicious rubbish.

He was so discouraged that he let his trot slow to a walk. Even at home, he was always hungry, but he needed extra energy to be able to travel. Right now, he didn't have any at all. He was even having trouble finding any puddles or streams today. He walked along with his head slumped and his tail hanging down. He had gone so far, and there was still no sign – or scent – of his family. He was *never* going to find them. It was hopeless.

Soon, he came to a very tall chain-link fence. It was much too high for him to climb over, even if he hadn't been so worn out. Besides, there were strands of nasty sharp wire at the top. But when he peered through the fence, he could see that the ground on the other side was smooth and even. It looked much more comfortable than the streets and pavements he had been on most of the afternoon.

He wandered along the fence to see if there might be a hole. As soon as he found one, he quickly crawled through. There were two long metal tracks with smoothly-packed earth on both sides. The tracks ran as far as he could see in either direction. He liked the fact that there didn't seem to be any cars around, so he decided to give this route a try.

He wandered north along the train tracks for a while. Once he passed a cement platform with a small building behind it. There were people with suitcases waiting on the platform, but none of them even noticed him as he slunk by. That was fine with him!

He walked and walked and walked. Sometimes the embankment next to the tracks was too steep, and he found it easier to walk on the tracks themselves. But he liked the embankments better, because they were softer, and there were no metal bars to trip on.

He heard voices, and stopped short, all of his

senses alerted. Was that danger ahead? Should he try and escape? Realizing that the voices were young, he relaxed. They were *boys*. Boys – and girls, of course – were his friends!

Feeling a little spurt of energy, he picked up his pace. It might be fun to walk with the boys. Besides, they might lead him to a place where he could find Gregory!

The three boys were friends from a nearby elementary school. Their names were Harold, Carver and Jason, and they were all in the fifth grade. They weren't allowed to walk on the train tracks, but they did it almost every day, anyway. They had always heard that train tracks were very dangerous, and their parents had ordered them never to go near the area, but the boys didn't believe it. If no one was supposed to be on the tracks, how come the fences surrounding them had so many holes? Besides, they were sure nothing bad would happen to *them*. Unless, of course, their parents found out, and then they would all get grounded – probably for years!

Santa Paws caught up with them without much trouble, barking happily.

"Hey, check it out!" Harold said. "Pretty neat dog!"

They all gathered around Santa Paws to pat him, and see if he knew any tricks. Santa Paws cooperatively shook their hands, rolled over, and even played dead for a minute.

"Cool," Carver said. "Wonder whose dog he is?"

Jason felt the thick fur around the dog's neck. "No collar or anything. Maybe he's lost."

"Maybe his owners are really mean, and he ran away!" Harold guessed.

"So, let's see if he'll follow us," Carver said.

The boys continued along the tracks, with Santa Paws trotting right behind them.

"I know my mother won't let me," Jason said, "but maybe one of you guys can take him home."

The other two boys looked at each other doubtfully.

"Well – maybe," Carver said. "I don't think my parents would want another dog, though. We already have two."

Harold just shrugged. His family had three rabbits, a guinea pig and some fish, so he wouldn't even bother asking for permission, probably. He knew they would say no.

"But it'll still be fun to play with him for a while," Jason said, and his friends agreed.

From somewhere down the tracks, there was a rumbling and a loud whistle. The boys didn't even seem to notice, but Santa Paws stopped right away. It sounded like a *really big* truck. It sounded bad. Maybe this wasn't a very good place to travel, after all.

"It's OK, dog," Harold said, and patted his back. "We always wait until they come pretty close before we jump out of the way."

"Yeah," Jason said enthusiastically. "Trains don't scare *us*. We think it's fun!"

What it was, was a very stupid and dangerous game. Trains were so fast and powerful that it took them a *very* long time to stop. Even if the driver noticed a car or a person on the tracks, by the time the train would be able to stop, the obstacle would have long since been run over. There was no such thing as a *safe* way to walk across railroad tracks. The only sensible thing to do would just be to stay away from them at all times.

The train chugged closer and closer. From a distance, it was impossible to tell how fast it was going. So it was easy to be fooled into thinking it was moving much more slowly than it really was. Santa Paws could feel the vibration of the carriages through the tracks and he moved nervously over to the embankment. He didn't like this place at all any more, and wished he had never crawled through that hole in the fence.

"What a baby," Carver scoffed.

The boys waited on the tracks until the train was so close that its whistle was almost deafening.

"OK," Harold shouted. "I count to three, and then we run!"

His friends nodded, grinning wildly. They liked "playing chicken" with trains. They had heard of other kids getting hurt, or even killed, that way, but they *knew* it would never happen to them. Not a chance.

"One!" Harold counted. "Two! Three!"

With that, he and Carver scrambled up on to the embankment and out of the way. Jason started to follow, but he slipped. He tried to get up, but found that he couldn't for some reason. He looked down and saw that his foot had slid underneath one of the sleepers. He tried to yank himself free, but his ankle was too tightly – and painfully – jammed between the hard-packed ground and the thick metal bar.

He was stuck, and the train was speeding directly towards him!

"Help!" he screamed. "Somebody help me!"

Santa Paws was terrified of the monstrous machine bearing down towards them, but he would never ignore a cry for help. He leapt off the embankment and down on to the tracks. Jason was trying to get up, but his lower leg was pinned in place by the sleeper. He was so scared he started crying as he tugged helplessly at his rapidly-swelling ankle with both hands.

Up on the embankment, his friends began crying, too. The train was going to hit Jason, and if they went down there to help, they would be run over, too. Why hadn't they listened to their parents, and just walked home safely along the pavements? Now it was too late!

The train whistle was so loud that Santa Paws was having trouble thinking clearly. The driver could see that there was something on the tracks, and put on the brakes. But the train had too much momentum, and it would be impossible for him to stop in time.

Jason cried harder and fought to get free from the rail pinning his trainer. Santa Paws yanked on his jeans leg with his teeth, but the boy's foot didn't budge. So he fastened his jaw around the trainer itself and shook his head back and forth fiercely. He would *make* that ankle come loose! The dog was able to tear away a few shreds of rubber, but it wasn't quite enough to set the boy free. So he dug fiercely at the cinder-packed ground under the sleeper, using both paws.

The train was almost upon them now! There was an earsplitting metallic screech as the driver pressed on the brakes with every ounce of strength he had. But the train just kept hurtling forward.

If Santa Paws jumped now, he would have just

enough time to be able to save himself. Instead, he stayed on the tracks with Jason, still using his strong front paws and teeth to try and prise the boy's foot loose. The train was so close now that he could actually feel the heat from the engine. At the last second, he gave up and dug his teeth into the back of Jason's ski jacket, instead.

Using all four of his legs for leverage, the dog tugged backwards with one great, twisting wrench. Jason's foot popped right out of his trainer and he fell backwards with a gasp of pain. Using more power than he knew he had, Santa Paws yanked him off the track and dragged him to safety, just in the nick of time!

Jason cringed as the train roared past them. Santa Paws was scared, too, but he kept his body protectively between the boy and the thundering machine. He yelped when stones and hot cinders flung up by the train's speed struck against him, but he never moved.

Up on the embankment, Carver and Harold weren't sure if Jason had escaped because the train was blocking their view. They didn't want to look, anyway, because they were too afraid of what they might see.

About a hundred metres down the track, the train finally ground to a noisy halt. Immediately, conductors and other railroad workers jumped off. They ran back down the tracks, terrified that they had just run over a young boy.

Carver was the first one to be brave enough to peer at the spot where his friend had been. All he could see was – a badly mauled trainer. Then he saw the big dog stand up from the space between the north- and southbound tracks. The dog shook his coat free of cinders and then nudged a weak and trembling Jason to his feet.

"The dog did it," Carver breathed. "He saved him!"

Jason just stood where he was, crying. He had sprained his ankle, but other than that, he was perfectly fine. Santa Paws ushered him firmly across the tracks and over to the relative safety of the embankment. He growled deep in his throat, because he didn't like it that the boys had been playing such a bad game, and wanted to warn them never to do it again. He knew now that railroad tracks were not a place for *anyone* to walk. Since the boys were still all crying, he hoped that they knew it, too.

There were lots of people racing towards them, and the dog didn't like *that*, either. They all seemed upset, and some of them looked angry, too. Since Santa Paws was feeling a little dazed and groggy himself, he didn't really want to be near yet another crowd of yelling strangers. He was *tired* of strangers.

The men and women from the train were overjoyed when they discovered that the little boy had somehow managed to escape. They had been *sure* that a terrible tragedy had taken place.

"Do you realize what a close thing that was, young man?" one of the conductors asked sternly. "You could have been killed!"

Jason – and his friends – nodded meekly.

By now, the local police had been summoned and two officers were climbing down to the tracks from their squad car. When they heard about the near accident, they got angry, too.

"You boys are going to ride home with us," one of the officers said. "Each and every one of your parents is going to hear all about what happened here today!"

Jason and his friends nodded, looking guilty. They had been expressly forbidden from ever setting foot on these tracks, and their parents were not going to like hearing that they had been disobeyed. The boys would probably be grounded – and they knew that they deserved it.

"You're just very lucky you got away in time," the other officer said grimly.

"It wasn't luck," Jason mumbled. "The dog saved me."

The adults all frowned at him.

"What dog?" one of them asked finally.

"The Alsatian," Harold explained. "He pulled Jason free."

Now the adults looked puzzled, as well as annoyed.

"I don't see any dog," one of the police officers said, sounding very suspicious.

Confused by all of this, Jason and his friends looked around the embankment and tracks.

The dog had disappeared!

Chapter 13

Santa Paws was very, very tired. He had taken advantage of the confusion at the train tracks to escape through a hole in the fence. Then he had run away until he couldn't go any further. Now all he wanted to do was collapse somewhere and get some sleep.

Many of the houses he passed were covered with bright holiday lights, and often a cheery Christmas tree was visible through the front windows. Other than sadly noticing the appetizing smell of suppers being cooked, the dog didn't pay attention to anything else.

He found a small playground and limped inside. The sun had long since gone down, so the park was empty, of course. When he had been struggling to free the little boy, the cut on his paw had got much bigger. It was throbbing now, and he felt as though gravel had got stuck inside the wound. It hurt a lot.

The playground had a sandpit, and he wearily climbed inside. Then he fell asleep almost before he had time to lie down.

It had been a very long day. He was glad it was over.

During the night, it began to snow. The dog moved from the sandpit to underneath the slide. Small flakes pelted him from both sides, but he was sheltered from the full force of the storm. Even so, it was very cold, and despite his thick brown fur, he could feel himself shivering.

By morning, at least fifteen centimetres had fallen, and the snow was still coming down lightly. Santa Paws gazed out at the wind-blown drifts covering the playground. Normally, he liked snow, but today it just seemed like another burden. The thought of plodding along through all of those drifts made him feel tired all over again.

He licked up some of the snow to soothe his dry throat. Eating snow made him feel even colder, but it was better than nothing. Then he crawled out from underneath the slide. The snow was the light, dry kind, as opposed to the wet, sticky type. That made it easier to walk, but hard ice crystals quickly formed around his paws. He had to stop fairly often, to chew them away.

Most of the streets had been cleared, but road salt had been sprinkled everywhere. The salt made the cut on his paw burn – and his other paws began stinging, too. So Santa Paws avoided the roads as much as possible. That meant he had to climb over uneven drifts, which was very strenuous. In no time he was panting.

When he turned a corner, he saw a McDonald's. He sniffed the air eagerly and his mouth began watering. Eggs, and bacon, and other wonderful odours! Forgetting his fatigue, he galloped over to the restaurant. One of the workers had just been emptying the rubbish, but he ran out of bags and went back into the restaurant to get more. In the meantime, he had left several sealed bags piled up near the wheelie bins.

Without worrying about whether it was bad, Santa Paws immediately tore one open. It was full of discarded food! He began gobbling the remains of Egg McMuffins, pancakes, sausages, and other breakfast foods. There were even some small cartons with milk left inside, and he slurped up as much as he could.

"Hey, you!" a voice called out.

Santa Paws wagged his tail pleasantly and went back to eating.

The young man, Wayne, who had been empty-ing the rubbish earlier, was frustrated to see that some of it was now strewn across the snow. But he liked dogs, and didn't really want to yell at this one.

"Come on, buddy," he said patiently. "I've got work to do here."

Buddy! Gregory sometimes called him Buddy! Santa Paws wagged his tail, and gulped down the remains of some hash browns.

Wayne had to laugh. *His* dog was a pig, too. "Go on home now, boy, OK? Good dog." Then he bent down to start cleaning up the mess.

Although there was still food inside the bag, Santa Paws stepped back politely. The boy didn't seem angry with him, and he wanted to keep it that way. But it was sad to see all of those tempting bags being tossed up into a wheelie bin well above his head. It was *wasteful*.

Deciding that he wasn't going to get any more food, Santa Paws turned to go. He barked a friendly bark, and trotted away. Once he reached the street, he had to turn around a few times to get oriented. Then, once he was confident he was heading in the right direction, he started off. With a little food in his stomach, he was in a *much* better mood.

A family of five was just leaving the drive-in window in their Subaru. They were the Kramers, and they were on their way to Rhode Island to visit their grandparents for Christmas. Mr and Mrs Kramer wanted to go up a couple of days early to help with the baking and decorating. They had three little girls. Janice was twelve, Gail was nine, and Susan had just turned four. For a special treat, their parents had decided to start their trip off with a quick stop at McDonald's.

Gail was the first one to notice the large brown dog moving steadily along the side of the road. "Look!" she said, so excited that she spilled most of her orange juice. "That's Santa Paws!"

Her father glanced at her in the rearview mirror. "Are you a sleepyhead this morning? You mean, Santa *Claus*."

"No, I don't," Gail insisted. "It's Santa Paws. He's magic!"

"Santa Paws!" Susan said happily, although she really didn't know what they were talking about.

Janice twisted around in her seat until she could work out where her sister was pointing. Then she saw the dog, too. His ears made him look like he was flying, so she recognized him right away. She had seen his picture in newspapers and on the Internet, and once on a cable news station. Even though this dog looked pretty scruffy, he was still very distinctive. "Hey, you're right," she said. "That *is* Santa Paws. Stop the car, Dad!"

Their father was utterly confused. "What on earth are you talking about?"

"Santa Paws," Janice repeated herself, speaking extra slowly. "The famous dog. The hero. *You* know."

"He's *America's* dog," Gail said solemnly.

"That's right," Janice agreed. "How can you not have heard of him, Dad?"

"I don't know," Mr Kramer said defensively, and then he looked over at his wife. "Have you heard of Santa Paws?"

"Of course," Mrs Kramer answered as she sliced a pancake into manageable pieces for Susan. "I thought everyone had."

"Yeah, really, Dad," Janice said. "You have to start spending more time online. He's all *over* the Internet."

Mrs Kramer nodded, since she had seen a couple of messages about the famous lost dog, too. "It's also been in the papers since he got lost," she said. "Pull over, David."

Mr Kramer shrugged and stopped the car at the side of the road. Janice and Gail unbuckled their seatbelts so quickly that Gail spilled what was left of her orange juice. Then they jumped out of the car, with their mother following close behind.

"Santa Paws!" Janice shouted. "Come here, Santa Paws!"

The dog stopped dead in his tracks. *Santa Paws?* Had he just heard his name? Puzzled, he lifted one paw out of the snow.

Gail clapped her hands a few times. "Come on, Santa Paws!"

Children. As always, he liked children. And if these people knew his name, maybe they knew the Callahans! Santa Paws ran over, wagging his tail. The girls were patting him, and he raised his paw to shake their hands. They thought that was pretty cool, and they patted him some more.

Mr Kramer stayed right by the car so he could keep an eye on Susan. Susan was interested in the big brown dog, but she was more interested in her breakfast.

Janice thought for a minute. "On the website I saw, it said to call the Oceanport Police Department. Up in Massachusetts."

"Why don't we bring him to Rhode Island?" Gail suggested logically. "Then his family can come and get him."

The Kramers stood and debated all of this, since their car was quite crowded. Finally, Mr Kramer was overruled, and it was decided that Santa Paws would come to Rhode Island with them. They would call the Oceanport Police Department on the way, and see what to do after that.

"He really needs a bath," Mr Kramer said, still uneasy about all of this.

"Of course he does, Dad," Gail said. "He's been *lost*."

"We'll just leave the windows open a bit," Mrs Kramer decided. "Come on, Santa Paws."

When Santa Paws realized that they wanted him to get into the car, his legs stiffened. This family seemed very nice, but the *last* time he had got into a car with strangers, very bad things had happened to him.

"Santa Paws!" Susan said, and waved a little piece of sausage at him.

Santa Paws instantly forgot all of his reservations and leapt into the back seat. Sausage was one of his very favourites!

"All right," Mrs Kramer said, once everyone was safely inside the car, and she was sure that her daughters were wearing their seatbelts. "Let's go and find a telephone, and then get on the road. We have a long drive ahead of us."

Santa Paws wasn't sure what was going on, but it felt good to be with a family again. He would just stay here for a while, and wait to see where they went. Besides, Susan still had some sausage left, and she might share it with him.

What he didn't know was that he was on his way home!

Mr Callahan heard the happy news from Uncle Steve about an hour later. He quickly called the high school and the middle school to let the rest of the family know what had happened. Santa Paws had been found!

Mrs Callahan arranged to let someone else teach the rest of her classes that day. Then she drove over to the middle school to pick up Gregory and Patricia. The plan was for the whole family to drive down to Providence, Rhode Island, to meet the Kramers when they arrived. Then they would get their adored dog and drive him back to Oceanport. Santa Paws would be home for Christmas!

They were all so excited that everyone talked at once as they drove. A joyous reunion was ahead of them, and they could hardly wait.

"I knew the Internet would help," Gregory said with a huge grin on his face. "I just knew it!"

Patricia looked worried. "I hope he's OK. Did they say he was OK?"

Mr Callahan shrugged. "According to Steve, the Kramers said he was just fine. They found him on a road in Connecticut, heading this way."

"So he *was* coming home," Gregory said proudly.

"He was certainly trying," Mr Callahan agreed.

The family drove down Route 128 to connect to Interstate 95. None of them could stop smiling

– or talking. In a few hours, their dog would be back where he belonged. All of their hopes and prayers had been answered, after all!

The further the Kramers drove, the more nervous Santa Paws got. Where were they going? Why was it taking so long? They kept patting him and saying words like "family" and "home". He liked the Kramers, but he had his own family. The last thing he wanted was to live with a *new* family, no matter how kind they were. So he whined deep in his throat, and fidgeted around in the back seat.

The dog loved riding in cars, but he was feeling too tense to look out of the windows. Every time he saw the scenery flashing by, it seemed as though his chances of finding the Callahans were becoming even more unlikely. This family could be taking him *anywhere*!

"He seems really nervous," Janice said. "Do you think he's carsick?"

"He's probably just tired," Mrs Kramer guessed. "He must have had a pretty rough week."

"I suppose so," Janice said, not quite convinced. "But – he's acting funny."

Gail patted the top of his head. "It's OK, Santa Paws. You'll be home soon."

Santa Paws managed a polite wag of his tail,

but the word "home" sent another chill of fear down his spine. He only had *one* home. Going to a different one would be awful.

The car stopped once, so that Mr Kramer could get petrol and Mrs Kramer could take Susan to the toilet. When the back door opened, Santa Paws tensed, getting ready to jump.

Gail put her arm around him to hold him back. "Sit, Santa Paws."

He obeyed automatically – but he didn't like it.

Soon, the family was back on the road again. Sometimes they sang Christmas carols, and sometimes Mrs Kramer handed out snacks. Santa Paws felt so edgy that he didn't even eat the oatmeal cookie Gail gave him. He was much too worried to be hungry. Riding in the car made it too hard to keep his sense of direction, and he had no idea where they were going. With each passing kilometre, he felt more and more anxious.

After what seemed like years to the dog, they drove into the city of Providence. Seeing tall buildings and concrete, Santa Paws began to panic. They were in a city! They weren't supposed to be in a city. He didn't *live* in a city. He didn't want to hurt the Kramers' feelings, but there was no way that he was going to be able to stay with them. He was going to have to run away, the first chance he got.

The plan Uncle Steve had arranged was for the Kramers to meet Gregory, Patricia, and their parents in front of the Trinity Square Repertory Company in downtown Providence. It was a landmark both families knew well, and it was small enough so that they would have no trouble finding one another.

Mr Kramer was driving towards Trinity Square when Susan announced that she needed the toilet again.

"Are you sure you can't wait?" he asked.

Susan was quite sure.

"It'll only take a minute," Mrs Kramer said. "Besides, we're here a little early."

Feeling the car slow down, Santa Paws sat up alertly. Were they about to stop? He hoped so!

"That's right," Janice told him. "We're almost there."

Santa Paws wagged his tail absentmindedly as he watched the street outside. Yes, this was definitely a city. It also did not seem at all familiar. Where in the world had they taken him? This was just terrible!

Mr Kramer stopped the car in front of a small, family-run restaurant. Gail was going to hold on to Santa Paws while her mother took Susan inside. But she changed her mind at the last minute.

"Wait, I'm coming, too," she said. She opened the back door and climbed out of the car.

In the split second before she closed it again, Santa Paws vaulted out after her. He needed to escape, so he could get back on the road and find his family. He looked at the busy street apprehensively, but then picked a direction at random and started running.

"Hey, wait!" Gail protested. "Come back, Santa Paws!"

Janice joined her on the pavement. "Come on, Santa Paws! Please?"

The family had been very sweet to him, and he paused just long enough to turn and wag his tail at them. Then, with a farewell bark, he loped gracefully away.

Mr Kramer, Janice and Gail tried their best to catch him, but the dog was too fast. Within a block or two, it was as though he had just melted away into the city. They kept running for several more blocks, but then regretfully gave up.

They had done a wonderful thing by finding Santa Paws – but now, unfortunately, he was lost again!

Chapter 14

The Callahans had never met the Kramers before, but when they saw a sad-looking family waiting in front of the Trinity Square theatre, they knew that something must have gone wrong.

"Where's Santa Paws?" Gregory asked nervously. "I don't see Santa Paws."

Mr and Mrs Callahan exchanged glances, both of them expecting the worst.

"Well, maybe he's in the car, Greg," Mr Callahan said, trying to sound optimistic.

Since they could see that all three of the Kramer girls looked miserable, that wasn't very likely. Mrs Callahan parked the car, and they quietly got out. Gregory clenched his fists and Patricia kept swallowing over and over, as they prepared to hear bad news.

When the Kramers told them the unhappy story, Gregory and Patricia couldn't believe it. They had come *so close* to getting their dog back, and now he was gone. It didn't seem possible. Neither of them could think of anything to say, so they just smiled weakly at the Kramers and tried not to start crying.

Their parents thanked the Kramers profusely for everything they had done, and for trying so hard to bring their dog home. The Kramers felt very guilty about the way things had turned out, but Mr and Mrs Callahan assured them that it was no one's fault. After another few minutes of conversation, the two families exchanged subdued Merry Christmases, and went their separate ways.

"They should have kept a better eye on him," Gregory said grimly, once the Kramers were gone.

Mrs Callahan put her arm around him. "They did their best, Greg. I'm sure he just got scared, because he didn't know where they were taking him."

Gregory only shrugged, and rubbed the back of his hand across his eyes. Patricia was so stunned and upset that she hadn't said anything at all the entire time.

"Let's get back in the car," Mr Callahan said.

"We still have a couple of hours before it gets dark, and we'll just drive around and look for him. Come on, everyone."

The rest of the family followed him without much enthusiasm. Santa Paws had got a big head start, and he could be anywhere by now. They knew that finding him in the middle of Providence would be a long shot, but they had to *try*.

Once Santa Paws was sure he had got away, he ran into an empty car park to catch his breath. He had to take the time to work out which direction he wanted to go. He had a strange sense that the Callahans were fairly close by, but he couldn't imagine where that would be. Or why. He was *sure* he had never been to this place before, and there was nothing that reminded him of Oceanport. It wasn't as scary and crowded as that other city had been, but there were still too many buildings and too many cars for him to feel safe.

The car park had been cleared, but it was still very icy. The dog sat down in a small, soot-stained drift to think. He sniffed the air for a long time, searching for something – *anything* – familiar. There were lots of city smells, like car exhaust and rubbish, but now he also noticed a distinct trace of the sea. He was somewhere near the ocean! That was good!

His instincts felt very confusing, because part of him wanted to travel north, and part of him felt pulled back in the other direction. That didn't make any sense, and he rested his head on his front paws for a minute. Why did he feel so torn?

North. He *knew* he wanted to go north. As far as he could tell, the conflict he felt was probably that he was sorry he had made that nice family feel unhappy. He just hoped they understood that he lived somewhere else – not this city, and his real family *needed* him. It was time to be on his way.

Santa Paws stood up, shaking away some loose snow. He had had a good long rest in that car. Now his legs felt strong and powerful again. He gave the air one last long sniff, and then trotted out of the car park. He had to turn a couple of corners before he was sure he was going in the right direction.

Then, running with a comfortable, steady gait, he headed north.

Providence was smaller than he expected, and he soon found himself on the outskirts of the city. His journey took him down streets with three-storey houses, and through old industrial areas.

He stayed well to the east of the big motorway, but followed in the same general direction. There were some train tracks, too, but he knew better than to go near *them*. Once was more than enough!

Darkness was falling, and he liked the protection that gave him. Other than the Callahans, he didn't want anyone else to get a chance to recognize him. *Ever again*. It was much too dangerous. For all he knew, that nice little family had taken him *kilometres* out of his way. He wasn't going to risk having that happen twice.

Some of the roads had too much traffic, but he had learned a lot about using traffic lights and flyovers to help himself safely avoid cars. The big streets still frightened him, but not as much as they had a few days earlier.

How long had it been since he had seen his family? He had no idea, but it felt like *years*. It would be so nice to curl up on his rug in front of the fireplace in the living room. He would be nice and warm, and someone would probably give him a Milk-Bone! Remembering what it was like at home made him feel so forlorn that his fast trot slowed to a walk. Now all he wanted to do was go somewhere and lie down and lick his sore paw.

Mournfully, he pressed on. Tonight he was noticing happy Christmas lights and other holiday decorations. Being by himself at this time of year seemed even sadder, somehow. He almost stopped to howl for a while, but just whimpered quietly to himself, instead.

He noticed a car up ahead of him slowing down. Cautiously, he stepped into the shadows of a hardware shop that had closed for the evening. Did the people see him? Was it the nice people? Was it the *bad* people? He waited against the side of the building, preparing to run away if necessary.

Someone on the passenger's side of the car opened the door and dropped what looked like a sack in the gutter. Then the door slammed shut, and the car drove away. Santa Paws didn't know what to make of that. How strange people could be!

When he was sure the car was gone, he ventured out into the street. He had a lot on his mind, but he was still curious to see what was in the sack. Maybe it was food! With that thought, he broke into a run. The nice family had given him lots of snacks, but that was several hours ago. Now, he was hungry again.

As he approached the sack, he saw that it was moving. He stopped. What if it was one of those nasty little animals with the bald pink tails? Yuck! He took a tentative step forward, then sniffed.

Well, it didn't *smell* like one of those ugly rodents. In fact, it smelled familiar.

The sack was an old pillowcase, with a knot tied tightly at the top. Whatever was inside was writhing around and making a small squeaking noise. No, wait, it wasn't squeaking.

The sound was more like – it was a *cat*!

Santa Paws woofed gently, hoping that the cat would relax. It would be much easier to free her if she weren't flipping around like that. Finally, he just rested a heavy paw on the squirming animal. That worked pretty well, and he began chewing a hole in the corner of the pillowcase. Once he got started, the cloth tore easily. He created a good-sized opening and then lifted his head out of the way.

After a short pause, a young black kitten stepped delicately out. The kitten took one look around and then swatted Santa Paws right on the nose. All of her tiny claws were extended, and the blow stung. But, more than anything, the dog's feelings were hurt. He had gone to all the trouble of saving this cat, and all he got in return was a vicious swipe across the face? It didn't seem fair.

Pleased to have established her dominance, the cat promptly sat down between the dog's out-stretched paws. Then, with tremendous dignity, she began to wash. She was a beautiful kitten, about eight months old, with silky black fur and yellowish–orange eyes.

Santa Paws was dumbfounded. Even though he had lived with one for a long time, he didn't understand cats at all. As far as he was concerned, they were *mean*. His pride was so badly wounded that he got up to leave.

In a flash, the kitten switched from dignity to charm. She began to purr loudly and rub her head against the dog's legs.

Santa Paws wasn't fooled for a second. As far as he was concerned, this little cat was only *pretending* to like him. If Santa Paws relaxed, the cat would probably turn right around and smack him again. Anyway, he had saved the kitten's life already, so now he was free to go on his way.

Seeing him start up the street, the kitten fell into the gutter and began to mew pitifully. Santa Paws tried to ignore the crying, but he just couldn't. With a deep sigh, he turned to go back. The kitten stopped crying at once, and purred energetically.

Santa Paws knew that the kitten really *should* be upset. After all, some mean people had just tossed her out of a car and abandoned her on a dark, snowy street. Gently, he nosed her out of the gutter and up on to the pavement. She would be much safer there, out of the road. He was sure someone kind would come along soon and give her a new home.

As he straightened up, the kitten swung her paw back and – wham! – scratched him again. The dog growled at her just loudly enough to show that he was irritated. The kitten's orange-yellow eyes seemed to brighten with mischief, and then – whack! – she let him have it one more time.

Very annoyed, Santa Paws headed up the street. He didn't feel like spending the rest of the night getting scratched. As far as he was concerned, that little feline could just fend for herself.

The kitten let out a terrified squeak and scampered after him. The dog barked sharply at her and kept going. But it would take more than *that* to discourage this stubborn kitten. Every time the dog looked over his shoulder, he saw the little cat trailing along behind him.

Santa Paws was very tempted to break into a run, and see if he could leave her behind. But this kitten was cute, and brave, and he was starting to like her in spite of himself. So he paused long enough to give her a chance to catch up. Then they trotted down the street together.

Whether he liked it or not, Santa Paws now had a travelling companion!

*　*　*

Having the kitten along slowed the dog's progress a great deal. The little cat wasn't used to the cold and snow, and she was finding it hard to keep up. Also, some of the drifts were so deep that they were almost over her head. They had to stop and rest much more often than the dog would have liked. Each time, the kitten would snuggle up against his body for warmth. It was nice not to be alone any more, but she certainly was making things difficult!

It had taken for ever, but they were now out of the city and into the quieter suburbs Santa Paws preferred. The kitten was complaining with hunger, so Santa Paws tipped over a couple of dustbins for her. He was happy to eat anything that seemed edible, but the cat was much more particular. She picked through the rubbish, tasting a morsel here and a morsel there. The dog had always thought that as long as it was food, it was just fine.

Every instinct in his body was urgently pulling him north now. Santa Paws had hoped to travel all night, but he wasn't sure the kitten could handle it. At home, Evelyn the cat never went outside at all. The dog wasn't sure, but maybe cats were only happy inside houses. This little kitten certainly seemed cold and tired.

He was able to urge her forward for another couple of hours. Then she plopped down in the snow and refused to go any further.

Except, they were right in the middle of the street! Did she really think they were going to sleep *here*? It was a pretty deserted road, but still. The houses were spread fairly far apart here, so it was more like the country than a suburb. Off in the distance, the dog could smell some farmyard animals like cows and horses and sheep. There were a few small farms in Oceanport, and he wondered if he might actually be near home. But he couldn't smell the sea, so he knew that these were different farms. He wasn't surprised, but he *was* disappointed.

If the dog had been alone, he would have dug a deep hole in the snow and used it for a nest. But somehow, he knew the kitten wouldn't be satisfied with that. He could see what looked like an empty building further down the road. If they were lucky, he would be able to find a way inside.

The kitten complained with a fierce meow when he used his paw to boost her to her feet. Santa Paws ignored that, already on his way down the road. The kitten followed him cooperatively, although she was so tired she kept slipping.

The building turned out to be a small house that was under construction. The walls and roof had been completed, but the inside was an empty shell. It was pretty well boarded-up, but there were plenty of pet-sized openings. The dog led the kitten inside through some torn plastic sheeting. He promptly stepped on a nail and yelped in pain. This time, he had injured one of his *back* paws.

The kitten had already found a comfortable place to sleep on some piles of insulation which hadn't been installed yet. Santa Paws yanked the nail out of his back foot with his teeth and then limped over to join her. The kitten reached her paw out, and he flinched instinctively. But, to his surprise, the kitten just patted him affectionately on the nose. Then she curled into a tight little ball and went to sleep.

Now that they were in out of the cold, the dog realized that *he* was pretty tired, too. He yawned widely and turned around three times. Then he arranged himself carefully next to the kitten, and closed his eyes.

When he woke up some time later, he wasn't sure what had disturbed his peaceful sleep. He blinked his eyes in the darkness, waiting for them to adjust to the light. Was there an intruder? Were they in danger? The kitten was still sound asleep, all tucked up against his side.

The dog lifted his ears and listened for any unusual or disturbing sounds. *Something* was wrong, but he wasn't sure what it was. He could hear crackling, and horses neighing. Then, as the smell of smoke filled his nostrils, he understood what the problem was.

Somewhere nearby, there was a fire!

Chapter 15

Santa Paws sprang to his feet and dashed towards the ripped plastic. The kitten mewed in protest, wondering why her new friend was leaving her so abruptly. Santa Paws just tore out of the house and began running towards the smoke.

For lack of a better idea, the kitten scurried after him. She really didn't want to be left alone in the middle of nowhere!

There was a burning barn across a field a couple of hundred metres away. Santa Paws vaulted over a snow-covered stone wall and into the field. He could hear panic-stricken horses neighing from inside the stable, and see the bright glow of flames burning through the barn's roof. He could also see a house, but all of its lights were off. The owners must be asleep.

At first, Santa Paws ran to the back door of the house and began barking. He scratched his paws against the door and barked, but no one came. OK, if the people weren't going to wake up, he would have to try to save the horses by himself.

Santa Paws turned his attention to the barn. As far as he could tell from the mixture of scents in the air, there were four or five horses inside, and they all sounded terrified. The fire had started somewhere back in the area where the hay and oats were kept. It was spreading so quickly that the smoke was even thick *outside*.

The barn doors were closed and Santa Paws pushed against them with all his might. But they didn't move. He moved back to give himself a running start, and then slammed his body against the doors. They *still* didn't move.

Then he felt the bite of small claws as the kitten ran right up his back. He was going to shake her off, but he could see that she was trying to reach something. He stood up on his hind legs, resting his front paws against the doors. Now she was high enough, and the kitten used her paw to flick the latch open. Then she jumped lightly to the ground.

With the doors unlatched, Santa Paws thrust himself forward again, pushing as hard as he could. When he backed off for a second, the kitten stuck her paw in the crack between the two doors and pulled one of them towards her. They were doors that needed to be *pulled*, not *pushed*.

Santa Paws took over now, using his body to open the door she had loosened for him. Great gusts of smoke came billowing out at them. Santa Paws took one last deep breath of fresh air and rushed inside the inferno. Although he didn't notice, the kitten charged in right after him. Most of the barn's roof had burned away, and the flaming support beams were starting to collapse.

The horses were whinnying frantically and kicking at the stall doors with their powerful hooves. This time, there were no latches. Instead, the stalls seemed to be secured by heavy wooden bars. Using his front paws, the dog was able to knock each bar free, one after the other. At first the horses were so scared that they didn't realize they could escape now.

Santa Paws used his muzzle to prod each stall open, and the horses began bursting out. So many hooves were flying around that he ducked to the floor to try and avoid them. In its panic, one of the horses kicked him right in the flank. It hurt so much that Santa Paws fell down. He picked himself up, keeping all of his weight off that leg.

A beam came crashing down right behind him, and he knew it was time to get out of this nightmare. It was *past* time. But as he staggered out of the fire, he heard a tiny meow coming from inside. He spun round and dived back into the fire to find the kitten. When she couldn't find a way to help Santa Paws, she had hidden underneath a small trough so that none of the horses would trample her. But then, when the burning beam fell down, it had blocked her escape.

The beam was on fire, but Santa Paws shoved his shoulder against it, anyway. He couldn't leave the kitten alone in the middle of the blaze. He moved the heavy beam just far enough for the kitten to scramble out from underneath the trough. Then the dog used his mouth to scoop her up from the ground. He carried her to the main doors, and then he lunged outside just as the rest of the beams came crashing down. The entire barn was on fire now, and the structure was already almost completely destroyed.

Santa Paws wanted to lie down in the snow to cool the burn on his shoulder, but he saw the horses racing back and forth like maniacs. If he didn't round them up, they would probably all run away. He dropped the kitten into a soft drift a safe distance away and then galloped after the horses. He barked his meanest, toughest bark to get their attention. It took a while, but he was finally able to herd them together.

The trouble was, he wasn't sure where to *take* the horses. The house had a double garage and he decided to guide them over there. The horses were restless and frightened, but Santa Paws ran back and forth and barked whenever they tried to move away from the garage. So they stayed where they were and whinnied a lot.

There were headlights out on the road now, and he could hear sirens, too. His first thought was that it was *about time* some people had shown up. But then he had to concentrate on the horses. One of them was trying to wander off, and since he was pretty sure it was the one who had kicked him, he snapped at it. The horse swiftly retreated to stand with the others. Santa Paws barked a more amiable bark in response.

The owners of the small farm, Mr and Mrs O'Neil, had been at a small holiday party at their neighbours' house. Someone had looked out of the window at one point, and noticed the flames. The entire party had rushed outside to their cars and headed straight for the farm. One of them had used a mobile phone to call the fire department, too.

Since it was obvious that the barn had been completely consumed, Mr and Mrs O'Neil were afraid that their beloved horses must have perished in the blaze. So, it was quite a happy shock when they swerved into the drive – and saw all five horses right there waiting for them.

"Oh, thank God," Mrs O'Neil breathed. "It's a miracle."

"No," her husband said, "it's a *dog*." He pointed at the large, smoke-stained Alsatian who was running from side to side, keeping the horses together.

Once all of the people started getting out of their cars, Santa Paws relaxed. It was *their* turn to worry about these crazy horses. The fire engines were already setting up out on the road. Some of the firefighters sprayed water on the back of the house to protect it from catching fire. The rest of them concentrated on what remained of the barn. Satisfied that everything was under control, Santa Paws went to find the kitten. He was worried that she might get scared and run near one of the cars.

"Whose dog *is* that?" one of the neighbours was asking.

"Gotta be a farm dog," another guessed. "How else could he herd like that?"

"Here, boy!" Mrs O'Neil said. No matter whose dog it was, she wanted to thank it for saving her beautiful horses. "Come here, you good dog."

Hearing "good dog", Santa Paws – naturally –

wagged his tail. The black kitten had climbed out of her drift and tottered over to meet him. This whole incident had been really stressful for her. Santa Paws licked the top of her head, and she rubbed against his front legs. Then they both headed across the field to go and get some more sleep.

"That was – strange," one of the neighbours remarked.

"That was – an *understatement*," one of the others said.

Everyone watched in disbelief as the dog and the kitten ran off together.

"Merry Christmas!" Mrs O'Neil shouted after them, since she wasn't sure what else to do.

The dog wagged his tail, and that was the last thing any of them saw as the two animals vanished into the dark night.

Fighting the fire had been so strenuous that Santa Paws and the kitten had to spend the rest of the night, and most of the next day, sleeping to regain their strength. Some workers arrived at the construction site early in the morning. Luckily, the dog and kitten woke up in time and were able to slip out between two boards before anyone saw them.

So they rested in a small gully further down

the road. Santa Paws dug down through the snow to make them a nest. The kitten was reluctant to lie directly in the icy snow, but finally she settled down. The snow felt very soothing to the dog, as it cooled the burn on his shoulder and the bruised lump on his leg where the horse had kicked him. Both injuries were painful, but he knew he was OK because he could still walk pretty well. He just wanted to get *home*.

They slept until almost dusk. Sometimes cars drove by, but they were far enough off the road so that no one saw them. Once it was dark, they yawned and stretched and climbed to their feet. The kitten shuddered as she shook snow off each paw. She really didn't like being outside like this. It was too cold, and too wet.

Santa Paws checked for traffic, and they stepped out into the street. When they passed the farm where the fire had been, they could hear the sounds of saws and hammers and other tools. During the day, much of the burned debris from the barn had been cleared away, but the whole area was still a charred mess. The horses were nowhere in sight, so they must have been staying somewhere else.

There was another small farm about a kilometre down the road. The dog and the kitten sneaked into a field where a few cows were, and drank some of their water. The cows seemed to be eating things like hay and grain from a wooden trough, which didn't appeal to the dog and kitten at all. Santa Paws tried a tiny bit of the grain, but then spat it out. It tasted like – cow food.

Santa Paws got the kitten as far as the next town before she started slowing down. He was never going to get home if she kept refusing to walk for very long! He tried to urge her forward, but she just mewed her most pathetic mew. They were behind a small parade of shops and the dog could smell food. He sniffed each building until he located the source. It was a Chinese restaurant, and tantalizing odours were streaming outside through a metal vent.

The kitten parked herself in front of the vent, and made it clear that she planned to stay there indefinitely. Santa Paws decided to find her some food, so she might behave better. The lid of the closest wheelie bin was too heavy for him to lift, although he tried several times. So he sat by the back door of the restaurant and barked.

The door opened, and a cook wearing white looked outside. Santa Paws barked again, cocked his head to one side, and lifted both front paws in the air. The cook said something in a language he didn't understand, and then added "No!" and "Go home!" in English. Before he had a chance to close the door, the kitten strolled over and started purring and winding around his legs. Then she sat down next to Santa Paws, still purring.

The cook couldn't resist *two* begging animals. He shrugged and stepped inside for a minute. He returned with two paper plates, which were sagging with the weight of rice, beef, chicken and even some shrimp. He set the plates down on the snow, shook his head, and went back to work.

The kitten instantly took charge of all the shrimp. Santa Paws didn't care, since he was happy enough eating everything else. Once he ate a hot pepper by accident, and *that* was a surprise. But he gulped down some snow, and soon his throat stopped burning. He resumed eating, but spat out any peppers or bits of orange peel he found.

The kitten gobbled her shrimp. Then she stuck her head in the dog's plate so she could nibble some chicken, too. Santa Paws was going to growl, but then just switched plates with her. She had left all of her rice and most of the beef.

When the kitten was full, she began playing with a stray pea pod. She batted it back and forth, and pounced on it once in a while. Santa Paws took advantage of this to lick both plates clean.

With her stomach warm and full, the kitten wanted to take a nap. But Santa Paws couldn't relax until they had gone at least a couple more kilometres. The kitten was sulky, but she followed him. Because she was taking her time, the dog had to keep checking to make sure she hadn't got lost. It seemed strange to him that she had no urge to hurry.

They came to a rest area near the big motorway. The kitten scampered underneath a picnic table where it was nice and dry. She yawned one of her big yawns, curled up in some frozen leaves, and went to sleep.

After exploring the terrain to check for danger, Santa Paws joined her. The rest area had a wooden information booth, which was closed, and there was a long line of pay phones. Other than that, there wasn't much to see. Occasionally a car or van would pull into the area. Sometimes a person would get out and make a phone call. Other times, the drivers seemed to be taking naps.

Feeling relatively safe under the table, Santa Paws decided not to worry about the infrequent visitors. There wasn't much chance that anyone would sit down for a picnic on a cold winter night! He kept watch for another hour or so, and then closed his eyes. Feeling responsible for another animal, not just himself, was really tiring!

* * *

The next morning was Christmas Eve. Santa Paws and the kitten, of course, didn't know this. The only difference they could see was that many more cars were driving in and out of the rest area. Lots of people seemed to be on trips today!

Santa Paws wanted to glide off into the woods, so they could avoid any trouble. Predictably, the kitten had other ideas. A truck had parked near their picnic table. The man driving went to make a phone call, and his wife disappeared inside the information booth. The kitten took advantage of this to run and jump on to their rear bumper. She gave Santa Paws a wicked look with her bright orange eyes. Then she sprang into the back of the truck!

Santa Paws got very upset. Why would the kitten be that stupid? Obviously, she would rather ride than walk, but these were strangers! This was a *very bad* plan. Didn't she understand that this truck would take them somewhere far away, and they would be even more lost than they were now?

The kitten poked her head up from the bed of the truck and blinked at him. Santa Paws knew the people might come back any second now. If the kitten was going to do something dangerous, he probably had to keep her company. But he was *not* happy that she was being so silly. At this rate, he would *never* find his way back to the Callahans.

The dog shot out from underneath the picnic table and sailed into the back of the truck. There was a loose tarpaulin covering the suitcases and other cargo stored there. The kitten had already climbed underneath, and he reluctantly did the same. He hid just in time, because the man had now finished his phone call and was walking towards them.

The man got into the driver's seat to wait for his wife. She came out of the information booth with two cans of soft drinks and some packets of peanut butter crackers. Once she was in the truck, her husband started the engine. He flicked on his indicator light, and then merged with the motorway traffic.

Crammed next to an overstuffed duffle bag, Santa Paws couldn't stop worrying. The contented kitten was already asleep inside a bag of Christmas presents. Once again, the dog didn't know where he was going, or how long it would take.

The *next* time the kitten got any bright ideas, he was going to let her go by herself!

Chapter 16

The truck sped up the motorway for a long time. Riding in the back was very bouncy, and every time they hit a bump in the road, Santa Paws bounced against the truck bed. Soon, his whole body felt bruised and achy. When he felt the truck slowing down, he poked the kitten with his nose to wake her up. If the truck stopped, they were *absolutely* getting off.

The truck pulled into a parking place, and the engine died down. Then Santa Paws heard both doors open and slam shut. Good! They could leave now!

Just as he and the kitten popped out, they saw the driver of the truck staring at them. The man had noticed that the tarpaulin in the back seemed loose. So he wanted to tie it down before going inside the restaurant for lunch. Santa Paws wagged his tail at the man before he and the kitten jumped to the ground. Then he and the kitten trotted out of the car park.

Not sure what was taking her husband so long, his wife came back to get him.

"Come on, James," she said. "Our table is ready."

James looked at his wife, still feeling as if he might be seeing things. "A dog and a cat just got out of the back and ran off together," he said slowly.

"Boy, your blood sugar must be *really* low," his wife said. "Come and get something to eat."

"But I *saw* them," James insisted. "Really."

His wife looked worried. "If you're that tired, I think I'll drive after lunch, OK?"

James nodded meekly. He looked around the car park, but there was no sign of any animals. It must have been his imagination – or low blood sugar.

By now, Santa Paws and the kitten were standing at the next corner, in front of a petrol station. The dog was trying to get oriented to yet another unfamiliar place. He knew which direction north was, but it just didn't feel right any more. For some reason, he wanted to go *south* this time. It didn't make sense. It seemed almost as if they had gone too far, and now he had to retrace their tracks.

The kitten was bored, so she started playing with her tail. It was fun to chase it in one direction, and then turn around and try to catch it from the other side. She was having a nice time.

Santa Paws took a few steps north, then paused. North had been the right way to go for *days*. Why did it seem wrong now? His instincts were telling him south, and east. It was cold, but the sun was out, and he looked up at the sky. Then he closed his eyes to think.

OK, southeast. They would go southeast. He would just keep trusting what his instincts – and his heart – told him. The kitten had stopped playing with her tail, and now she was swatting *his* tail. The cars in front of them had stopped for a light, so it was safe to cross. Santa Paws used a paw to propel the kitten forward and lead her across the street. He wanted to cover as much ground as he could before she rebelled again.

They trotted, or walked, all afternoon. Santa Paws began to smell the sea, which gave him some confidence. Maybe southeast really *was* the way to go.

He took the cat through building plots and gardens as much as possible. They found some good leftovers behind a McDonald's, and were able to drink at a small pond later on. When the kitten started yawning, he carried her by the scruff of the neck for a while. At first, she liked it. Then she began yowling, and he put her down. The snow was deeper here than it had been where they were before. He could understand why she was running out of energy, since he was losing steam, too. But the smell of the sea kept getting stronger, and that made him feel good. He was *sure* that they were going the right way now.

In the early evening, they stopped for a nap. The kitten picked a spot underneath a pine tree. It was fairly dry and soft under there, and the dog liked the smell. He thought about the Callahans, and their funny habit of bringing trees into the house. Would they find his family soon? He was so tired and achy that he wasn't sure how much further he would be able to travel. And he *knew* the kitten couldn't handle much more. But he missed them – more than anything.

He and the kitten cuddled up together, and went to sleep. When an unusual sound woke him up later, the dog didn't want to open his eyes. He only wanted to rest. But then he heard the noise again. It seemed to be a woman, and she was groaning.

So the dog hauled himself to his feet and trudged off to find out what was going on. Seeing him leave, the kitten glumly went after him. She took her time, lagging about five metres behind.

Santa Paws followed the sound to a small ranch house. A woman with a huge stomach was sitting at the bottom of her front steps in a daze. She kept holding her stomach, and moaning.

The woman was Wendy Jefferson. She was eight and a half months pregnant. Her husband had gone out to do a few last-minute errands before the shops shut. Right after he'd left, she'd gone into labour, and she was afraid that her baby was going to arrive at any second. Her contractions were only a minute or two apart! She had called 999, but the ambulance was taking a very long time to arrive. So she'd gone outside to try to get into her car and drive to the hospital. Now the contractions were so close together that she was having trouble getting up, so she was stuck here, alone, at the bottom of her steps. She was going to have to deliver her own baby!

Santa Paws woofed once, to let her know he was coming. The lady seemed upset, and he didn't want to scare her.

"Help," Wendy gasped, between contractions. "Please help me!"

Santa Paws certainly knew *that* word. As he turned to alert the neighbours, the kitten meowed curiously. The dog lifted her up and put her down next to the woman, to keep her company. Then he ran over to the house across the street. Christmas carols were playing loudly inside. He barked and barked, but no one seemed to hear him.

So he went on to the next house. A retired couple was home, watching *It's a Wonderful Life*. The husband, Mr Thompkins, came to the door. Santa Paws barked and pulled him outside.

"Careful there now, fella," Mr Thompkins warned him. "I'm not too steady on my feet. What seems to be the problem?"

Santa Paws barked, and ran towards the pregnant woman's house. Mr Thompkins was intrigued enough to follow. When he saw his neighbour lying on the ground, he was horrified.

"Lou, the baby's coming," Wendy said in a weak voice. *"Right now."*

Mr Thompkins nodded and turned towards his own house. "Molly!" he bellowed. "Call an ambulance! Wendy's baby is coming!"

"Oh, my!" his wife responded. Then she ran to the phone.

Everything seemed to be OK now, so Santa Paws scooped the kitten up. They retreated to the edge of the property, just out of sight, to watch until the dog was *sure* it would be all right to leave.

Wendy's husband and the ambulance arrived at the same time.

"What happened?" her husband asked, looking worried. "Are you all right?"

"The baby's coming," Wendy answered, between the special breaths she'd learned at her natural childbirth classes. "A dog went and got help. At first, I thought it was Santa Paws, but he had a cat with him."

"Oh, it couldn't have been Santa Paws, then," one of the paramedics said authoritatively. "He works solo."

Everyone else nodded. That was a well-known fact about Santa Paws – who, before he had been stolen, had lived only a couple of towns away.

From the bushes, Santa Paws and the kitten sat quietly and watched all of the excitement. The baby was coming in such a hurry that the paramedics had to deliver him right there on the front steps! They didn't even have time to carry Wendy over to the stretcher! It was a beautiful baby boy, and he cried a loud, healthy cry. Quickly, Wendy and her new son were bundled into the ambulance. Then her husband climbed in after them with a big grin on his face. The ambulance drove away, sirens wailing, and Mr and Mrs Thompkins went back inside to watch the end of their film.

Now that the big event was over, the kitten yawned widely. She was ready for another nap! Santa Paws sighed, but then gave in. He wouldn't mind another couple of hours' sleep, either.

So they returned to their pine tree and nestled together again.

It was late that night before Santa Paws could persuade the kitten to get up. Every place they walked, people seemed to be sleeping. Except for Christmas lights, and street lights, it was very dark. There were no cars driving about, which made it very easy to get around. Santa Paws and the kitten wandered right down the middle of each street, where there was the least snow.

They walked until morning. Santa Paws steadily guided them southeast the whole time. The smell of the sea was very strong now, and he stopped to fill his lungs with the aroma. It made him feel very homesick. He was so tired that all he could concentrate on was placing one sore foot after the other.

The only thing that kept him going was the thought of seeing his family again.

At the Callahans' house, it had been a quiet Christmas morning. In fact, since their terrible disappointment in Providence, it had been a very quiet couple of *days*. Gregory and Patricia's grandparents had driven down from Vermont, and of course, Uncle Steve, Aunt Emily and their daughter, Miranda, had come over, too. Gregory and Patricia didn't feel at all like celebrating, but they were trying to be good sports. All they said were things like "please" and "thank you" and "excuse me".

"Where's Santa Paws?" Miranda kept asking. She was so little that no one had really been able to explain it to her.

"Why don't you open this pretty red parcel?" Aunt Emily suggested, to change the subject.

Miranda happily tore off the wrapping, but then looked up at everyone else. "But *where* is Santa Paws?"

Gregory and Patricia took that as a cue to go to the kitchen and bring out a fresh coffee cake. Really, they just wanted to leave the room for a minute.

"We, um, we got some pretty nice presents," Patricia said.

Gregory nodded, since they *had* got lots of really terrific gifts. "Do you think Mum and Dad would mind if I went upstairs for a while?"

Patricia knew exactly how he felt. She wanted to do exactly the same thing. "We can't yet," she said. "Not with Grammy and Grandad here, and everything. Maybe after lunch."

Gregory sighed, but nodded again. He had never imagined that Christmas morning could be such an ordeal. Even with lots of guests, the house just seemed so – empty.

Patricia put on an oven glove and took the warm coffee cake out of the oven. She slid it on to a plate, and Gregory carried the cake out to the living room.

"You know, your mother and I were thinking," Mr Callahan said, from the rocking chair near the fireplace.

Gregory and Patricia both froze. Their parents weren't going to suggest getting another dog, were they? They didn't *want* another dog. *Ever.*

"Maybe we could drive back up with your grandparents and do some skiing this week," Mr Callahan went on. "Would you like that?"

Gregory and Patricia loved to ski, but the idea didn't sound as exciting as it normally would.

"That sounds great," Uncle Steve said, his voice extra-enthusiastic. "You can try out that new snowboard, Greg, and you've got those great glacier glasses, Patricia."

"Yes," Gregory said, making an effort to smile. "That would be fun."

"Yeah," Patricia agreed. "I mean – thank you."

Their parents smiled, but their eyes looked very sad. Uncle Steve had only been trying to cheer them up, so he just shrugged helplessly and drank some coffee.

Gregory and Patricia sat back down on the sofa. They still had lots of unopened presents left, and Patricia hadn't even touched her stocking yet.

Miranda stopped banging on her new toy drum for a second – which was a relief to everyone in the room. "Why is the cat crying?" she asked.

They all looked over at Evelyn, who was sound asleep by the fireplace. Then everyone looked at Miranda, with some confusion.

"Well, sweetpea," Grandad said. "She's fine. See how she's sleeping?"

Miranda shook her head firmly. "She's *crying*. The cat is very sad."

Thinking about why Evelyn might be sad made Gregory and Patricia feel even worse. She probably *was* sad. And she wasn't the only one.

"Daddy, help the cat," Miranda said to Uncle Steve.

He was just as perplexed as anyone else, but he bent over to pat Evelyn. Before he touched her, Evelyn suddenly sat up straight, with her ears flicking forward.

"Hey, that's weird," Gregory said, hearing a pathetic little meow. "There *is* a cat crying." The sound seemed to be coming from the front door, and he got up to check. He opened the door, and saw a small black kitten on the welcome mat. Her legs were tangled, and it looked as though she had been plopped straight down from the sky.

The kitten stopped crying at once, and stood up with a big stretch and a yawn. Then she ambled past him, and into the house.

"Hey, whoa," Gregory said, stepping out of the way. "Weird."

"Is that your black cat?" Miranda asked Mrs Callahan.

"Well – apparently so," Mrs Callahan answered, with a small smile.

Miranda smiled, too. "Pretty cat."

The little kitten was marching straight to the kitchen. She found Evelyn's bowl right away and helped herself to some tuna-fish. She purred happily, and drank some water, too.

Gregory looked at Patricia. "That's totally weird. A cat just like, *showing up*."

"Maybe some elf left it," Patricia said wryly.

Gregory thought about that. After all, they hadn't heard a car or anything. But, no, even at Christmas, that would be unlikely. He started to close the door, but then stopped and stared outside.

"What?" Patricia asked.

"I don't know," Gregory said, feeling his heart

begin to beat faster. "I just – for a minute, I thought—"

They looked at each other and then threw the door all the way open. Their dog was running towards the house, wagging his tail, and holding the morning newspaper in his mouth!

"Santa Paws!" they said together, and then they raced outside to meet him.

Santa Paws was so excited that he dropped the newspaper. He began barking, and jumping, and trying to kiss them – all at the same time! Gregory and Patricia started patting and hugging him, and they all ended up sprawled in the snow together. Gregory and Patricia weren't sure if they were laughing, or crying – or doing a little bit of both.

"Mum, Dad, he's back!" Gregory yelled. "Santa Paws came home!"

Everyone in the house ran to the front door to see the joyous reunion. Mr and Mrs Callahan started crying when they saw their beautiful dog, and soon everyone else had tears in their eyes, too.

"*There's* Santa Paws," Miranda said, smiling broadly. "Santa Paws brought the cat for a present. Santa Paws *always* comes at Christmas."

Under the circumstances, none of the adults were about to disagree.

"It's a Christmas miracle," Grammy said softly.

With all of the hugging and the barking and the tears, it took a while before anyone was ready to go inside. Hearing the commotion, their neighbours up and down the street had come out to see what was going on. Realizing that Santa Paws – everyone's hero – had come home, they all started clapping.

"Welcome home, Santa Paws!" someone yelled.

"Merry Christmas, everyone!" Mr Callahan said, waving to them. "Come on over! We're about to have a *very* big celebration."

The whole neighbourhood thought that was a wonderful idea, and they all came trooping towards the Callahans' house. Someone started singing "Joy to the World". The rest of the neighbours – and Miranda – joined in.

Mrs Callahan, Aunt Emily, Grammy and Grandad went to make coffee, tea and hot chocolate. They also filled plates with homemade cookies and brownies for the group to enjoy. The neighbours filed into the living room, still singing. Uncle Steve was on the phone to the police department, so he could pass on the good news. Mr Callahan was putting fresh logs on the fire to keep the room nice and warm. All in all, it couldn't have been more festive!

Santa Paws sat on his rug in front of the

fireplace, right between Gregory and Patricia. He smelled of smoke, and motor oil, and who knew *what* else, but they were so happy to see him that they didn't mind at all. The only thing that mattered was that their dog had come home! The black kitten, who was already feeling like part of the family, lounged in front of them and purred. Evelyn examined the kitten, decided that she approved, and sat down nearby to wash.

Patricia and Gregory couldn't stop patting and hugging their dog. Santa Paws wagged his tail as hard as he could, and took turns shaking hands with them. Over, and over again.

"Hey, boy," Gregory said suddenly. "Do you want a Milk-Bone?"

Santa Paws barked with delight. *Yes!* He wanted a Milk-Bone! He wanted a Milk-Bone *very much*.

The room was filled with laughter and excitement and jolly conversations. Santa Paws couldn't believe that after so many long, lonely days, he was back on his rug, with Gregory and Patricia patting him. He looked at his family, his two cat friends, and the roomful of nice visitors. What a great time he was having! It was Christmas, and he was home safe and sound.

He had never felt so happy in his entire life!

And – he hadn't even eaten his Milk-Bone yet!